Choice, Set Free
Book 3

The Tae'anaryn
&
the Paladin's Squire.

By Dr Joseph Ireland, PhD.

"Dr Joe"

The Tae'anaryn and the Paladin's Squire

Published by Dr Joe – www.DrJoe.id.au

Ed 1 © Dr Joseph Ireland 2015 (was 9781518786631) Wombat books

Ed 2 © Dr Joseph Ireland 2018 (ISBN: 9781728987040) CS

Ed 3 © Dr Joseph Ireland 2018 (ISBN: 9780992329457) Spark

Ed 4 © Dr Joseph Ireland 2024 (ISBN: 9780645899924) Spark, colour

National Library of Australia Cataloguing-in-Publication entry

Author:	Dr Joseph Ireland "Dr Joe".
Title:	The tae'anaryn and the paladin's squire.
Series:	Choice, set free. Book 3
Imprint:	Dr Joe
ISBN:	9780645899924
Date:	15 October 2018
Pages:	252
Size:	140mm x 216 mm (5.5 x 8.5 in)
Spine Width:	14.503 mm
Weight:	325 gm
Target Audience:	Primary school age. "Middle fiction".
Subjects:	Individuality--Juvenile fiction.
BISAC:	YAF000000 Young adult fiction
Dewey Number:	A823.4 F IRE
Lexile Number:	750

Cover design and internal illustrations by Dr Joseph Ireland

By Dr Joseph Ireland "Dr Joe"

About the author

Hi, I'm Dr Joe, and I love telling stories.

Fantasy gives us a safe place to explore difficult issues, and I wrote this story to ask some of those hard questions not even science can answer – I hope you enjoy it!

I currently live in Brisbane, Australia, with the wife and three very talented daughters. I run a touring science show business to kindies, schools, and holiday programs, and fill up my spare time with storytelling – either writing books or running Dungeons and Dragons games. Life is pretty good!

Sincerely,
Dr Joe Ireland

More wonderful titles by Creating Science & Dr Joe:
Choice, set free.
Delightful high fantasy for the thoughtful young reader
1: The Quest of the Tae'anaryn
2: The Tae'anaryn and the Wizard's Apprentice
3: The Tae'anaryn and the Paladin's Squire
4: The Tae'anaryn and the Enchantress's Chrysalis
5: The Tae'anaryn and the Spear of the Troll Prince
6: The Tae'anaryn and the Khozmoh Djinn
7: The Tae'anaryn and the Voyage of Imagination's Dawn
8: The Tae'anaryn and the Crown of the High King

Engaging science fiction adventure with real science!
Space Chase 1: Arrendrallendriania
Space Chase 2: Elizabeth
Space Chase 3: Daniel
Space Chase 4: The Mechanizer
Space Chase 5: Moiya
Space Chase 6: Pancake

Dragon Riders of Pearl
Because Dragons…
Dragon Riders of Pearl 2: Seven Worlds
Dragon Riders of Pearl 3: Return of the Plague
Dragon Riders of Pearl 4: Rage of the Dragonmen
Dragon Riders of Pearl 5: Twilight of the Giants
Trilling young adult science fantasy adventure.

The world's best D&D campaigns – The Wolf in the Sky, Balor's Blade, Quill Versus the Lost Academy of Angelfall, and Hidden city of the Exiles

And don't forget – Creating Science, hands on science experiments and activities for everyone! And Dangerous Science, science to blow your minds.

iv   By Dr Joseph Ireland "Dr Joe"

Choice, set free 3: The Tae'anaryn and
The Paladin's Squire

by Dr Joseph Ireland
"Dr Joe"

Dedicate

For the angels that help us.

8,9,5,99,50,1,99,61 4,32 16,2,3 20,91,5,9 7,2,4 100,6,26,1,6,40,6 1,99.

By Dr Joseph Ireland "Dr Joe"

Contents

Table of images

     By Dr Joseph Ireland "Dr Joe"

Choice, Set Free

Characters

Kialessa – the hero of the story. She is a tae'anaryn, a race with a demon as one parent. She has red skin, small horns, and a tail. Few like her, and fewer trust her even if she *did* save the king's life once.

Darrix – one of her best friends, a prayerful warrior.

Piex – another of Kialessa's best friends, a wizard's apprentice.

Allastassia – a talented enchantress, and the most popular girl at the college.

Posk – Kialessa's best friend, a mentally disabled half-troll boy with exceptional physical strength and speed.

The kingdom of Lenmer'el

King Dunnkan – the kind king of the nation. His closest advisers and personal bodyguard consist of:

High Captain Bon Sure'e – the captain of the king's army and the strongest and most skilled warrior in Lenmer'el.

Lord Cour De'Feur – high wizard of Lenmer'el, an elf. National expert on things arcane, including the sciences of magic and alchemy.

Lord Grudon Fletcherson – the king's steward, in charge of running the day-to-day affairs of the kingdom.

Lady Jacinthia Stonehall – a dwarven priestess of the Eternal, and the highest religious authority in the kingdom.

 By Dr Joseph Ireland "Dr Joe"

Other characters

Lady Annadaria Greens'holm – Allastassia's mother. A powerful part dryad enchantress, arguably the most powerful in the entire Great Kingdom behind Sagesse L'aimé, Elven Queensage of the North.

Lord Tar Greens'holm – Allastassia's noble born father, known as a capable and intelligent diplomat. He raises his only child, Allastassia, with great indulgence.

Uncle Joesef – Allastassia's uncle, known for his ability to sleep approximately eighteen hours a day, often more.

Harrobar and Niania Minerson – Darrix's parents. Not born to wealth, Harrobar is considered a 'merchant prince' – a rising class of non-nobles who are gaining power in the Great Kingdom because they are rich and influential merchants. The noble class watches them with

1 Harrobar Minerson, Darrix's father.

wary uncertainty. Niania is known as a beautiful woman, who is also shy, anxious, and who avoids all social events wherever possible.

Doreth – a senior student, a dwarf. A capable cindersmith, or priestess of the dwarven god of the hearth and storytelling.

Patsi de Vere – the youngest daughter of a very wealthy noble human family who have lived in Lenmer'el since its founding 313 years ago. She has no particular gift or special talent, but is outgoing and friendly to all, and is one of Allastassia's oldest and closest friends.

Tomin – the most famous and skilled paladin of the entire High Kingdom. Paladins are deeply religious warriors, renowned for their integrity and virtue as well as their strength in battle.

2 Patsi De Vere, one of Allastassia's oldest friends

        By Dr Joseph Ireland "Dr Joe"

Glossary

Appointed – decided on beforehand.

Capitalise – to make profit from.

Confederation – a group of people that agree to cooperate and help each other.

Conflagration – a fire.

Congeniality – friendliness, good manners.

Constitution – the composition of something.

Cupid – someone who sponsors a romance.

Dexterously – skilful and competent.

Derisive – rude and unwelcoming, insulting.

Dissidence – rebellious behaviour.

Docile – sleepy and calm.

Edict – a publically announced law.

Elation – great joy.

Entourage – a group that follows someone around, typically with permission.

Faculty – ability or power.

Fawned – to show affection or attempt to please.

Fidelity – faithfulness.

Frenetic – rapid.

Fundamental – the foundation of something.

Hypocritical – doing the opposite of what you tell others to do.

Incinerated – burnt up.

Initial – first.

Inoperable – not functioning.

Jocular – comical.

Missive – message, such as a long letter.

Motif – a decorative image or design, typically with repeated patterns.

Nemesis – someone who is a direct challenge.

Oblivious – completely unaware.

Obstinacy – stubbornness.

Pantheon – a group of gods that belong together, even if they don't always get along.

Parapet – the top of a castle wall. It usually has special defences, such as narrow arrow slits, or holes for pouring boiling oil onto attackers.

Perspicacity – clarity of thought.

Piety – religious devotion and respect for the gods.

Placid – docile.

Protocol – official procedure for doing things.

Serendipitous – very lucky.

Skirmish – a battle, usually irregular or unplanned.

Swineherds – someone who looks after pigs – a very important job in cultures that like bacon.

Tendrilous – having tendrils (such as vines or liana).

Tyranny – cruel and oppressive leadership.

Unmitigated – unchanging or without equal.

          By Dr Joseph Ireland "Dr Joe"

Choice, Set Free

By Dr Joseph Ireland "Dr Joe"

The Tae'anaryn & the Paladin's Squire

By Dr Joseph Ireland "Dr Joe"

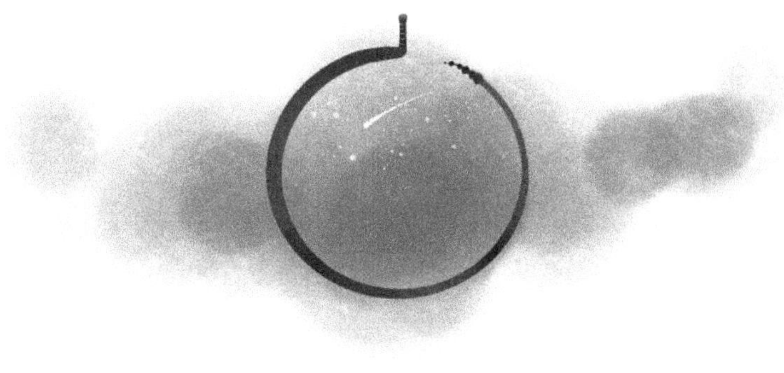

The curse

Change is power; embrace change.
Fear of change weakens you.
Embrace change; embrace power.
– High King Malkom, 15.2.313 CY.

Sharp cracking sounds echoed around the deserted streets, like iron hammers on tortured stone. She turned in the darkness and saw red sparks dancing up from the cobblestones at the rapid approach of a cloaked figure riding a tall, fierce beast. She could make out neither rider nor beast in the shadows, but they carried with them a powerful aura of unmitigated fear.

3 Messages in dreams...

Kialessa leapt back, pressing herself against the cold stones of a town building. She was in the village within the castle; that much she could tell. But how she came to be there, or what she was supposed to be doing, she had no idea.

The rider thundered down the street, sinister shadow-forms springing into being every time the sparks flew. He headed right towards her and there was no avoiding the bleak gaze that seemed to bore into her from the depths of the dark hood.

She reached for her weapons but found none. Even

By Dr Joseph Ireland "Dr Joe"

her father's treasured whip was missing. Her breathing quickened, her heartbeat thundered within. She was alone, curled up against silent stones.

With a horrifying cry the rider charged her, stalling his mount at only the last instant rather than crush her to death against the stones. The beast was tall and thin, shaped in a form she had never seen before. Its hooves were shod with iron and it wore some form of spiked armour about it. The rider was still cloaked in darkness so she couldn't see who it was, yet she couldn't take her eyes away from the darkness within that hood.

She felt, rather than heard, a voice. He spoke with only a whisper, yet it was a whisper of perfect evil and spite. *If you stand in my way, tae'anaryn, I will personally flail the skin off your bones.*

She could not stop trembling, desperate to escape. But it was not done talking to her yet. *Change is coming. Change is necessary. It is time for my master's cause to prosper. Stand aside, Protector, and let this be.*

Trembling, she could not speak.

I will not warn you a second time, the creature said and pulling on the reins of the mount, reared up. With a terrifying screech, the beast lashed out at the air.

Kialessa could contain herself no more, and gathering all her strength, she screamed.

Kialessa! Kialessa! the cruel being mocked.

Then the voice changed, becoming higher, less

threatening, more familiar. 'Kialessa, Kia! Wake up!' she heard her friend Allastassia shouting.

Kialessa opened her eyes, and found herself staring out at a room full of frightened students. She remembered then that she was in the girls' dormitory, in the castle of Lenmer'el. She found herself curled up at the end of her bed and her friend Allastassia was shaking her fiercely.

There were tears in her friend's eyes, 'Kialessa, what happened?'

'It's… all right,' Kialessa said, trying to shake the last threads of the dream from her mind, 'just a nightmare.'

'You were moaning,' Patsi, Allastassia's good friend said, clearly just as shaken as the rest of the people in the room, 'then that scream!'

'You would best a banshee,' said Doreth, a young dwarven cindersmith.

Kialessa tried to smile but couldn't bring herself to try very hard.

'Tell us,' Allastassia pleaded. Dreams were powerful. Dreams could be used as messages from the future, or the past. Dreams could be used to shape reality or to warn against what was becoming.

'It was all so vivid, but now I don't seem to remember anything,' Kialessa muttered, frustrated that the dream had slipped so quickly from her mind. 'Someone was trying to tell me something. To make me frightened. He told me to keep out of the way …'

        By Dr Joseph Ireland "Dr Joe"

'What did he look like?' Doreth asked, her huge hands clenched into fists as though she was already for a fight.

Kialessa shuddered as the evil of a few moments ago seemed to seep into the room with her reluctance to recall the being. The others grew nervous too.

'You don't suppose it was a message from a demon?' Patsi said with careless innocence.

At that suggestion, everyone made a ward sign or two against evil. Kialessa's hand almost instinctively reached up and held on to her memento of the Eternal, that her good friend Darrix had made for her.

Allastassia might have been about to speak but an adult's voice cut her off.

'Right!' said the old head mistress, keeper of the children, with enough conviction and authority to stall all conversation. 'Enough. No need to frighten yourselves anymore. Kia, we will talk of this in the morning with the priestess, if need arise. But the rest of you, back to bed!'

A moment later there were heavy footfalls at the door and two guards burst in. 'What happened?' one shouted. 'Is everything all right?'

'Yes,' the head mistress said in a tired voice, 'just a bad dream.'

'But that scream,' he muttered, checking his weapon. 'We thought hell had opened up and swallowed one of you!' History had records of it actually happening.

The old headmistress lit some sage twigs and began to

wave the smoke around the room. 'Nothing we can't handle, good soldier. Now take your unwelcomed presence from this room of the women before you bring a curse on *yourself*. Go! We are well equipped to handle this. And you girls, back to your beds! Don't let someone else's dream concern you. You each have enough of your own. Beds. Now.'

With some reluctance and anxiety, everyone took to their beds once more. Kialessa tried to snuggle down in her cotton sheets but even the lamb's wool rug didn't seem to hold enough warmth for her this night. As the hour drew on and the other girls fell asleep one at a time, Kialessa found herself still wide awake, praying for comfort in the quiet night.

'Are you asleep?' she heard a voice ask. It was Patsi, whispering to her from the bunk beside her own.

'No,' Kialessa replied.

'Do you think the dream meant anything?' she asked. 'Or was it just, you know, a meaningless fear?'

Kialessa sighed, unsure. 'I hope it didn't mean anything. I have these dreams sometimes. They tell me things.'

'Are you a dreamwalker?' Patsi asked with surprise in her voice.

'No, but I know someone who is.'

'Oh,' Patsi sounded a little disappointed. 'Did your dream come from them?'

'Definitely not.'

Patsi was silent for a while. 'Well, I hope it means nothing. It scared the life out of you and your scream scared the life out of everyone in the castle!'

'I'll try not to scream like that ever again.'

'Do your dreams ever tell you things about what's going to happen, like, in the future?'

'Usually they only tell me about what's happening right now.'

'Well, I don't think that's useful. I'd love to have dreams that tell me about the future or *something*. I never dream about anything interesting or useful. I'm pretty boring. Not like you Kia. You're so talented. You have skin that doesn't burn, you can walk on a rope, you have these… horns. And now I learn that you have dreams that tell you what's happening! It almost makes me wish I was a tae'anaryn. So talented …'

Kialessa was silent. Dreams that told her things that were happening when she could do nothing about them? Dreams that were so soon forgotten but were so terrifying they woke up an entire castle? That wasn't talented.

That was a curse.

On how to succeed in life and business

And what does it profit a man if he gains the whole world, through successful business, and loses his soul?

– Jacinthia, High Priestess of the Eternal at Lenmer'el. Sermon given 15.2.313 CY.

The little stone cutting tool went *plink, plink, plink.*

It was the next day, and Kialessa was watching, all bad dreams forgotten. She was sitting on a wooden stool in the stone crafting workshop, her tail swishing lazily in the dust that covered the floor and every other surface.

4 On how to succeed in life and business

There were only two others there that afternoon. Darrix was one of them. He was carefully striking a chisel with a mallet as he attempted to carve the little image into the stone that his father had requested.

The other person was Darrix's stern father. 'Keep breathing, son. Can't have you pass out on your first attempt!'

Kialessa could see that the older man was watching his son with affection, but his voice was serious and commanding.

Darrix took a deep breath. He was silent, brow creased in concentration.

'That's it, nice and slow. You need the patience of

Halm himself to turn stone into art, my boy.'

Darrix huffed. 'You know I don't take much to the old gods, Father. Like the king, I am of the Eternal-'

His father laughed. 'And what of it? Your people do and thus so do I; for it is what will sell. And in the end, success in business is to sell what people want to buy.'

Darrix continued to chip away. 'What about success in life? What does it profit a man if he gains the whole world, through successful business, and loses his soul?' he asked.

Kialessa recalled the saying from the teachings of the kind dwarven priestess who tended the shrine of the Eternal each Serrosday.

But Darrix's knowledge of the Eternal was lost on his irreligious father. 'And what good is a man so full of heaven he cannot feed his children?' his father quoted in reply. Darrix's father was a bulking human, almost a head taller than most other humans, with a thick chest and strong arms. He'd started life as a soldier, his two oldest children following his example. But his real strength lay in his cunning and hard work which had won him the mining rights of a profitable gem mine. Every Planasday, just like all the other youth, Darrix was forced to spend time with his father learning his future trade – gem and stone mining.

It was a business Darrix had next to no interest in ever learning, and Kialessa could see that this was a source of contention between the two of them. But what was one to do, when the father insisted the son become a great and wealthy merchant, but the son wanted only to serve a god his father could not see and did not care to learn about?

'A man "too full of heaven",' Darrix replied with a clever smile, 'would never let his family starve or go without. If he is too full of visions to feed his children, then they are not visions of heaven.'

The father huffed. Clearly he was not the sort to let his son deny himself the wealthy and prosperous future he intended for him. 'Be that as it may. You, Darrix, will not waste time at the shrine of any god when there is business to be attended to.'

'Then why bring me here?' Darrix asked, stretching out his back. 'I don't mind stone cutting, though I'm not really good at it. What about attending to the papers or seeing the trade caravan leaves on time?'

'I thought you'd never ask!' his father shouted, snatching the chisel from his son's hand and placing his hand on the stone image. 'Business, successful business is just like cutting this stone. You cannot simply wish it into form. You must plan, then commit to your plan, chipping away at your business again and again and again. Never too much, for if you try to rush you might offend a customer, cause a mine to cave in or lose a deal. In the same way, if you rush here you will split the stone and stand to lose a whole week's work. You must have patience, cutting away a small piece at a time. Stick to your original plan and never lose sight of the final goal. Don't rush. Use little taps, sharp tools and patience. *That's* how to succeed in business.'

'And in life?' Kialessa wondered out loud.

'Yes, perhaps, in life as well.'

The older man smoothed the stone and seemed reasonably pleased at his son's efforts, but then returned the chisel to see how Darrix would finish it.

Kialessa shook her head. *So that is why Darrix has been brought to the cutting floor,* she thought, *to listen to his father lecture him. Poor boy. It will be a looong morning for Darrix.*

Even so, a part of her envied him. He had a father who would take a day out of life just to teach him something. Her parents had all but ignored her until the day the king had decided it was time for her to start studying at the college.

Since it was Planasday, the day before they all took a day off from their studies for the week, the parents and tutors had arrived to take the students to their individual lessons. Yet Kialessa had nothing to do but follow her friends, for none had claimed her as their student or apprentice though she'd been at the college for almost half a year. Her first friend Piex was studying happily with the castle wizard Sagemaster De'Feur, reading entire tomes faster than Kialessa could make sense of a single page. Her other friend Allastassia was no doubt tending to the work of nobles or showing off her enchantress's talents.

     By Dr Joseph Ireland "Dr Joe"

They'd both allowed Kialessa along once, but she'd found it so tremendously boring she'd never been again.

Posk, the half troll, came and went as he pleased from the forest, so there was never any telling where he was or if he was coming into town. Kialessa had tried to follow him one Planasday, but there was just no keeping up with his frenetic movements in the wild. She'd lost track of him in no time and he seemed to forget she was even trying.

However, Darrix often found interesting things to do, so Kialessa had taken to watching him again today. And so she sat contentedly on a wooden stool in the stone crafting workshop, her tail swishing lazily in the dust that covered the floor and every other surface.

Darrix's father looked like he was drawing breath in preparation for launching into another lecture when there were shouts from outside. 'Eh, what's this?' he muttered.

They hurried to look out the workshop windows. Coming down the street in a great hurry was a formal-looking procession. At least a dozen guards from the High Kingdom were accompanying a purple and gold clad messenger on a dark furred posk. They lumbered down the main street with great haste, scattering citizens in their wake.

'Indeed,' Darrix said, as though wary.

'The High King's men!' his father answered. 'There are no feasts of which I am aware. There must be some urgent news!'

'You don't think there will be war?' Darrix asked, his voice serious.

His father huffed into his thin beard. 'Don't even speak such evil!' But he paused while he considered, muttering, as if thinking his thoughts out loud. 'Even so, the western trolls might be moving again, especially with the fall of that wizard Tobiuus you both know so much about.'

He glared at them, for Darrix had put himself in great danger without his father's permission to help rescue her from the tower of the corrupted wizard, Tobiuus. But he and Kialessa just grinned at each other.

'But I sincerely hope not,' his father continued. 'Would not be good for business, unless … anyhow. Young tae'anaryn here, what was your name again?'

'Her name is Kialessa, Father,' Darrix replied on her behalf before she could, sounding a little annoyed.

'Thank you, Darrix.' His father glowered at him. 'I hear you are good at sneaking around. Did you not once break into the Sagemaster's study?'

'How did you hear *that*?' Kialessa asked in surprise.

'Never you mind. But here's the thing – would you like to do your friend Darrix here a little favour?'

'Very much,' she said with a grin, but she wasn't sure whether his father was going to ask a favour for Darrix, or himself.

'Great!' he said, talking to her like she was a little child.

          By Dr Joseph Ireland "Dr Joe"

'You see, those emissaries from the High King are going to have something very, very interesting to say to King Dunnkan and it might be really, really important for us to know what that is. So if I can get us into the castle, do you think you can sneak into their meeting for me and tell me what they say, please?'

'That's not very nice,' she said, her grin fading.

'I'll give you a *silver coin* for your trouble,' he waved a coin in front of her face.

Kialessa huffed. She owned over twelve hundred of them already, and spying on King Dunnkan was not something she was going to be paid to do.

But she *was* willing to do it for free! She liked being the first one to find out things in the castle and it sometimes seemed like people would sneak her secrets just so she could pass the message on to the right person. And she had to admit, she was pretty good at it.

So she turned her nose up at the coin. 'I'll do it, but not for you. For Darrix.'

'Oh, you mustn't spy on the king for me, ever!' Darrix said.

'Son, don't be a fool. You must know that … running a business is like hunting,' he said as he hustled them out the door.

'I thought you said it was like cutting a rock.'

'It is! But it's also like hunting. You need to know how hunt a golden opportunity. Wait patiently, keep your ear out and listen closely. Then when you find it, shoot it right away! Don't delay, be the first to know. It'll earn you thousands of gold coins. I speak that from experience!'

'Yes, Father,' Darrix muttered in an unhappy tone.

Kialessa thought he looked sad at the thought of her sneaking in to listen to the king, but could probably see some his father's wisdom.

Kialessa, for her part, was very excited. She loved sneaking in on the king and listening to what he said. Actually, she loved sneaking up on anybody, from the cutlery maids to the well-dressed nobles. But especially, she liked to surprise King Dunnkan. She thought him a kind man who never rushed a decision, always spoke to everyone involved and always asked for advice even if he was the king. He'd talk to the wizard, to the steward, the captain of the guard. He even talked to the prisoners sometimes, but there wasn't time to recall that story right now.

So she didn't need Darrix's father to hurry them in through the palace gates. She knew she would be allowed there on her own as one of the king's friends, having saved his life recently. But being there with her friend's father meant the castle guards, who sometimes caught her sneaking around during the late afternoons, would be less inclined to shoo her away with an adult merchant beside her – a rich, 'noble', merchant prince.

It took five moments to pass through the enormous

gate houses in the two great walls that protected the glorious castle of Lenmer'el. It was more than a century old, having stood for sixty years before King Dunnkan came to rule at only thirty-two years of age. It had taken an entire decade to build, calling on the skills of both dwarf and human master artisans to complete. They approached the inner keep now, and Kialessa tried hard to ignore the imperious glares of the two massive sculptures of human knights that stood as though protecting the entire country. She often imagined they could bring their stone swords to life any moment and cut down entire forests in a single act of violence. In a world full of magic it was a real possibility.

At least they'd be on our side, she thought.

Darrix's father took them to the throne room, where statues of bronze blocked their way. Darrix's father turned to speak to a human guard, 'I wish to see the king.'

The guard looked annoyed, almost angry, 'You know as well as I do, Minerson, that you need to make an appointment with the steward. Why did you not send a messenger to his office? It is treason to enter here uninvited, even if you do have Dame Kialessa with you.'

'I know, I know,' Darrix's father made a placating gesture. 'The workers at the mines have been complaining about goblin raids. They are in fear for their lives, and I promised them I'd do everything in my power to ensure a *quick* and *immediate* response – ' he pratted on, but his emphasis on the words 'quick' and 'immediate' sounded like an unnecessarily obvious signal for Kialessa to slip away.

Darrix cast a worried look at her, but she smiled at him to let him know it would be all right.

She meandered out the way they came in. She ducked behind the arched window and look around. No one seemed to be here. She quickly climbed up the outside wall of the throne room like a monkey and slipped into a second story window. From there, she made her way across the balcony and hid behind a huge tapestry in the throne room. It was her favourite hiding place; she had found she could wait there for hours without anyone noticing her.

She peered out carefully; making sure no one – especially the wizard or his pet pocket dragon – saw her.

The room was full of royal guards. King Dunnkan's elite were armed and alert while at least six of the High King's men, soldiers of great skill themselves, waited. The messenger from the High King was standing out in his official gold and purple uniform.

The messenger fidgeted with his robe. He appeared to be getting impatient. King Dunnkan was nowhere to be seen.

The message

King Dunnkan will not be hurried in his own hall!
– King Dunnkan, castle records, 47.2.313 CY.

'Why does the King delay?' The messenger asked authoritatively but not rudely. He was tall; a pure blood elf, with light mauve hair and golden eyes. He was accompanied by three men at arms, clearly elite soldiers of Emerel from the look of their gilded swords and sigil encrusted armour.

The steward hushed him. 'King Dunnkan was not expecting to host any messengers from his Lordship, the High King today. He is preparing himself.'

'Granted, though I am under much pressure to deliver this message and return to his Lordship with King Dunnkan's reply to this important –'

'King Dunnkan will not be hurried in his own hall!' It was the king. His voice was lordly but not unkind. 'Especially if it is a message of great importance, as you say.'

'Indeed,' the messenger said, bowing low, 'and I meant no disrespect. I only intended to do the bidding of his High Lordship above all.'

King Dunnkan did not reply. He was a king, serving under a king. The High King ruled seventeen other kingdoms as a confederation of nations that protected each other. The High Kingdom had stood for over three hundred years now, many generations among humans, although hardly a lifetime to most elves.

King Dunnkan sat on his throne in his royal red robe. His queen and grandson, the eight-year-old crown prince, sat on either side of him. His most trusted advisors gathered around the throne. All of them waited to hear the surprise message from the High King.

King Dunnkan nodded to the priestess, who called down some kind of sanctuary on the outside of the tower. Kialessa was glad that she was already inside.

'There is no need for privacy,' the messenger declared. 'This message is to be broadcast immediately to all people.'

'Is that so?' King Dunnkan asked, his voice doubtful. 'It is not like the High King to declare matters publicly outside his own kingdom, except for matter of war.'

'Then indeed it is, if we count the war of the gods. Here reads the High Kings message: "To all people within the Great Kingdom – peace and honour and plenty. I, Malkom, eighth of the High Kings, protector and convenor of the High Kingdom, send forth this solemn decree to be observed in every kingdom, city and manor that call themselves under the protection of the High King. I solemnly proclaim that from this day forth, the gods of the old Pantheon are to be preferentially honoured in every house, city and kingdom within the High Kingdom. The deeds of the old Pantheon are to be spoken of in every public place on the fourth day –" '

'What is this madness?' King Dunnkan interrupted.

'Here, you may read it yourself. It bears the High King's seal,' the messenger said, with a polite bow. Kialessa could tell he knew his news would not be popular. The wizard took the message and quickly read over the three pages.

'What of the worship of the Eternal?' King Dunnkan asked, concern obvious in his voice.

'The High King has asked all shrines and symbols to any gods not of the Pantheon that are currently in public places or by highways, be taken down or removed. He expects the old Pantheon to be honoured above all so that we may expect their protection in matters of war and the far greater war of personal integrity. He asks that the sacred days of the seven gods be honoured –'

'This is unjust!' King Dunnkan stood up from his throne, his guards stepping forward in readiness. 'He cannot order religious segregation! He cannot mandate who his people worship, except in the cases where it harms others! What he's proclaiming is the exact opposite to the religious freedom we have enjoyed for over three hundred years! I … I …' He paced about, fists and jaws clenched, ignoring his queen's invitation to be seated.

'As I read the edict, your honour,' the wizard said, 'the High King is not disallowing the worship of any gods that are already legalised. He is simply asking for preferential treatment of the seven gods of the old Pantheon. I do not believe we are in any way in current breach of this proclamation.'

'Yes!' King Dunnkan almost shouted, pointing at the wizard as though already victorious. 'We already honour the holy days of all seven gods of the old Pantheon, and that officially.'

'But the High King does expect the High Kingdom to honour the old Pantheon above all other faiths,' the wizard finished.

King Dunnkan did not look pleased.

'If it be your will, my king,' the steward said with a disarming smile, 'there are things we could do to honour the Pantheon further. Let us renew the shrine of Lumos and perhaps do greater honour to the winter feast of Pumos.'

'Pah, that dark deity receives a mention at every funeral.'

'Be that as it may, perhaps I can find ways to honour the High King's edict without burdening the people or stripping them of their religious freedoms?'

King Dunnkan mumbled something under his breath. Obviously, others had more to say, but few would express their opinions in the presence of the High King's messenger.

'And I did notice,' the messenger said apologetically, 'a small shine to Theiss, goddess of roads on the way here. I expect such will be moved from the main highway?'

'What? No!' Dunnkan replied. 'I may not hold to the old gods, but my people do, and they built that shrine with their own hands in remembrance of a young boy who died there during a carriage accident!'

'Be that as truth,' the messenger said, 'perhaps it would be better moved to a lesser road, only to honour the High King who protects us all.'

King Dunnkan did not speak, but was clearly upset. The rest of the people in the room were silent.

'I have received the honoured High King's message, and will act on it immediately and in truth faith to the High Kingdom,' King Dunnkan stated, somewhat coldly, 'Now, if you're done, you must want to rest after your journey?'

'Indeed,' the messenger said with a deep bow, 'but I

am ordered straight back to the High King's presence.'

'Really? That seems odd. Is there war about?' King Dunnkan said.

The messenger bowed, avoiding the king's glance, 'None that has reached my ears,' he replied, though he sounded suspicious to Kialessa, 'but I do believe the High King desires only the unity and peace of the people.'

'As do we all,' King Dunnkan said with a voice that did not conceal his anger well.

The messenger bowed once more, as did his entourage, and they left. King Dunnkan took the message, and after trying to read it a moment, threw it on the floor. He sat on his chair and brooded. Kialessa was worried. She'd never seen him so troubled.

'This is does not feel right,' he whispered.

'Don't fear, my love,' the queen said, 'it is a simple message to obey and you need not leave the worship of the Eternal. We may assume so from the edict. We can do much to support the High King's command.'

'Quite so!' the steward agreed. 'It will be a small matter to command the people to honour the Pantheon. They already do!'

'Indeed, it seems almost mute,' the priestess pondered out loud, 'telling the people to do what they are already doing.'

'This does not feel right,' the king repeated quietly to himself, but no one had any answer. 'Steward, let's do this properly. I want you to write up a petition. Sign it in my name and in the name of the people. Let the High King know his unfair law *will be* protested in this kingdom.'

'Within the hour, your highness,' the steward explained, looking for all the world as though he was already planning what he was going to write.

The king sighed once more, 'As for the rest of us, well, I guess we'd better get to deciding how to implement the High King's edict appropriately. Suggestions, please? And don't mention that shrine to Theiss again. The poor mother places flowers there every single day. Besides, it reminds others to take that bend more carefully!' King Dunnkan managed a smile.

*This **is** interesting news indeed,* Kialessa thought. It took her a few moments before she felt safe enough to sneak out again and run back to Darrix and his father. She found them working in the stone cutting shop once more.

As soon as she saw them, she shouted out the news, 'The High King is demanding that everyone honour the old Pantheon!'

Darrix's father didn't waste a moment, but called a runner to him and begun issuing instructions. 'We must double the number of carvers at the stone masonry. Have them build statues as quickly as they can and pay them as much overtime as they like!'

Darrix was concerned. 'What exactly did King Dunnkan say?'

'He was boiling. He almost threw the messenger out right away!' She gave a broad smile. This was big news.

But Darrix was not smiling. 'That's not like King Dunnkan, to put out an official messenger from the High King. But I can understand his anger. If the High King puts away all gods not of the old Pantheon, the worship of the Eternal may be banned next.'

She'd heard King Dunnkan suggest as much, but Kialessa was still disbelieving. The government telling people what they were supposed to think and who they were supposed to believe in? 'The High King wouldn't do *that!*'

'Let us hope not.'

'But there'd be an uprising,' Kialessa said.

'Perhaps not as much as you might expect. But in any event, I don't think the High King would ban worship of any good religion. The High Kingdom was built on the ideals of religious and social freedoms. It would be strange indeed. But then … he is the High King.'

'You don't trust him?' Kialessa asked, wondering if Darrix was really going to speak ill of any king.

He huffed, and said instead, 'Well, it'll certainly be welcome news to the forty or so priests of the council of Serros here in Lenmer'el!'

Then they waited for a while, till it was obvious that Darrix's father would not be paying them any more attention that day. He was busy rushing around, finding

        By Dr Joseph Ireland "Dr Joe"

different ways to capitalise on the news he was first in town to know. He finished organising his workshop of statues and religious symbols to go into overload and then ran out, announcing to them all that he was on his way to purchase a shop of religious icons so that he could really get the most from his sales.

With nothing else to do they left Darrix's father to his business breakthrough and went to look for Piex. It was the afternoon, and he would sometimes take to studying outdoors at that time. Often he would practice casting, which sometimes required volunteers, and *that* was always a challenge.

Horses

When you put your life in danger you are left with two choices – learn from it, or die. Thankfully ... I can offer you both.

– The Demon Tyrant, circa 318 CY.

They found Piex on the wall above the front gate, watching the road as though he had nothing else do to.

'What news, Piex?' Darrix said.

'Oh! You guys. Yes, greetings.'

'Good afternoon, Piex,' Kialessa said with affection. 'What are you doing out here? We thought you'd be studying.'

'I am ... or I'm not.'

He wasn't making much sense to Kialessa. 'What?' she

       By Dr Joseph Ireland "Dr Joe"

asked, never afraid to let him know she didn't understand.

'Well, it's like this,' he said. 'When your wizarding master asks you to watch a pot boil, you watch the pot until it boils.'

'I see,' Darrix said. It sounded like he was also confused.

'Piex, start making sense,' Kialessa ordered.

That seemed to snap him out of his thoughts. He'd grown a lot since his imprisonment in his uncle's tower, but some things didn't change, like his occasional absentmindedness. 'Sorry. Master Coeur De'Feur is expecting a delivery of some "profoundly interesting life forms" this afternoon and has asked me the personal favour of watching at the gate and calling him when they arrive. And so it doesn't matter how boring the task is, if the master requests it, it gets done.'

'I see,' Darrix said. 'My father expects the same.'

'Really?' Piex asked, disbelieving.

'Really. Besides, I expect you found ways to entertain yourself.'

'True, I was re-reading the Sagemaster's treatise on regional flora. I'm grateful he's working on a second edition, given the many errors of the first,' he muttered, never intending to sound arrogant, but the fact still remained he was probably looking at the entire book in his memory. There were no books to be found lying around at the castle gate.

'Well, we're here now, so you can practice your casting if you like,' Kialessa said.

'Yes, please!' Darrix agreed, always looking for a challenge.

'Oh, I don't have any … look, what's that?' Piex said.

In the distance, rounding a bend in the road that led to the castle, came a strange procession. It was a great carriage, much the same as any the Posk might pull, but the beasts that bore it were creatures unlike any she had ever seen. Their image brought back a sudden flash of fear Kialessa could not place, but the feeling vanished just as quickly.

As the carriage drew closer, for truly the creatures were swift, they could see that they looked a lot like giant deer, only without antlers. Their backs were at least as high as a human's shoulder, their necks thick and strong. They had long, thin legs. Their fur, if they had any, was short, except for a long mane of hair that ran from the tops of their heads to their shoulders. They were all brown, though some had great white patches on them.

'What are they?' Kialessa asked in amazement.

'I have no idea.' Piex said. He immediately cast a spell that would alert his master: Bright flares of coloured light streaked up into the sky.

By the time the creatures had reached the gate the Sagemaster had come running, and the entire guard and

 By Dr Joseph Ireland "Dr Joe"

many citizens were flocking at the gate to look at the strange creatures.

The woman who rode them wore tight black clothes and a thin, round helmet. She stood boldly on her carriage and spoke to the wizard with a thick foreign accent. 'Noble wizard, please be informing of King Dunnkan that his *horses* has arrived!'

The crowd continued to marvel while she set up the strange beasts in a field that seemed to have been set aside for her arrival. Kialessa and her friends pressed up against the fence while they watched her unshackle them and prepare them for some kind of demonstration.

'Posk would love to see this!' Darrix said.

'Oh, yes!' Kialessa agreed. She began crawling backwards through the crowd. Posk was one of her friends from the school, a mentally disabled half troll boy who loved combat training and couldn't understand the point of reading. He lived in the forest near the castle, it seemed, and he never took off his magical gauntlets that the king had given him for helping to save his life earlier this year, but that was another story. They'd named him after the animal that pulled the farmer's plough, the posks, but no one had ever told her why. Posk the boy was green, and strong, and liked to pat other people just a little too often.

'Where are you going?' Piex asked.

'To get Posk!'

'You'll miss the demonstration!' Darrix shouted, but she was already off and running to the castle wall, the one that boarded onto the forest. She pressed past the guards as she ran up to the top of the lonely parapet.

There was a trick she used in training, one that had won them many battles, and also woken up half the castle when she had had a bad dream. Kialessa could shout loudly. Very loudly. Her voice would take on a strange sound, one that set people's teeth on edge but seemed to cut into the air a long distance.

'POSK!' she screamed to the woods.

The guards on the tower jumped but she ignored them. The forest was silent. Kialessa disregarded the half dozen guards disregarding their posts to watch her with curiosity and interest. The voice that came from her no doubt sounded so unlike the little tae'anaryn voice one might expect to hear.

'POSK!' she screamed again. This time, she thought she heard his bellowed reply across the distance, but she wasn't sure, so she waited half a moment …

'POSK!' This time he definitely replied. Within a moment she saw him running, sometimes on all fours, through the forest. He didn't stop once he reached the castle wall but scampered right up it like it was a ladder. He landed right beside her, gauntleted fists clenched and eyes wide, looking at her with concern.

She'd never seen anybody do that before. 'Wow,

how'd you run up the wall like that?'

''Lessa,' he replied, looking concerned.

'Oh, there's nothing to be worried about.' She knew he didn't have the language skills to answer any of her questions anyhow. 'I've got something I want to show you. Come with me.'

He followed her down the stairs then pushed passed her to run ahead, stopping often to see which way she was going. There was no outrunning Posk. She didn't put anything on his neck to 'harness' him as people were used to him now and knew that he didn't deliberately cause trouble.

They made it to the horses only moments before the king. Kialessa slipped her way dexterously through the crowd while people just bounced off Posk as he ploughed his way, reasonably gently, though. They flung themselves down on the ground besides Piex and Darrix, and found Allastassia sitting on a silk rug beside them both.

'Hey y'all! Everyone's here!' Kialessa said.

'Good evening, Kialessa,' Allastassia said, then added coldly, 'Posk.' She held a handkerchief to her nose and leant as far away from him as was possible.

He seemed oblivious to her disdain. He plonked down beside Piex, muttering some kind of tune to himself. Darrix patted him on the back but prevented him from returning the gesture. The half troll still didn't know his own strength nearly as well as Darrix did.

'As I was saying,' Allastassia continued, 'they're horses, from the blithling lands far to the far east. They're much faster than posks and only need grain to survive. They're a new creature.'

'Are they dangerous?' Piex asked.

'Quite. Some are bred for war, like posks. You think their teeth are too blunt to do much damage but they'll cut off a man's hand in a heartbeat, and their hooves are much more dangerous and faster than a posk's claws.'

'They're much taller than posks, too,' Darrix said, 'and that'll give them an advantage in battle, I imagine.'

'Are they obedient?' Piex asked.

'So I hear tell; as clever as dogs, really.' Allastassia spoke as though she'd done nothing but study horses all her life.

Posk seemed enchanted. He didn't take his eyes off them for an instant, his nose pressed up against the wooden fence. The woman was standing on one of their backs and riding in a circle, making them do all sorts of interesting tricks such as walking sideways, or standing on their back legs when she told them to.

'So why are they here?' Kialessa asked.

'King Dunnkan heard of them at the last kings' conference,' Allastassia replied, 'and has paid a fortune to bring them up here from the eastern lands to be demonstrated. I hope he buys them.'

          By Dr Joseph Ireland "Dr Joe"

Four of the horses were paraded around in circles. They seemed like bright and obedient creatures, not nearly as submissive as the posks, which had nothing better to do than follow orders. The assembled nobility and castle workers clapped their appreciation. Finally, King Dunnkan called for silence.

'Fine creatures you have there, baroness Emerald!' he called.

'The honour be mine, Majesty and Grace,' she replied in her thick foreign accent. 'You seem of good health for a land that hides its sun!'

He laughed. 'And you've arrived in good time, as you said you would. I am every bit as impressed as I expected to be at your beasts!'

'These horses,' she said like a professional saleswoman, 'will be the envy and honour of every kingdom around. You have been showing great wisdom in being the first of your peoples to see them. Each was trained in my home this year and will serve you well.'

'I haven't bought any yet!' he replied, in good humour. 'But I might, if they continue to impress me. What is your price?'

'Five thousand gold!' she said boldly, which brought no small stir from the crowd. 'Which includes my services for a year while your peoples be learning to love and train them!'

'That's more than a lifetime's wage,' Kialessa mused

in amazement.

'It's a year's for my father,' Darrix replied.

'We spent that much last week,' Allastassia muttered. Her parents were very rich.

'As did we …' Piex agreed sadly, though he was a wizard and would be lucky to see two coppers from the sales of magical goods he'd help craft. While an apprentice, all he made was considered property of his master.

'Five thousand!' King Dunnkan said, then paused. 'Very well, if you can impress me sufficiently.'

The baroness stopped as though she'd never had her first offer accepted before, and had expected the king to bargain for at least half that amount.

'But if King Dunnkan pays full price,' Allastassia explained, 'he can resell at a higher price too.'

The four horses were quickly saddled, and the baroness rode one across the field. It moved quickly, its feet making a sound like a muffled drum as they struck.

'Wise they be, and honest. Trained, they are to be a warrior's best friend. So, good King, who would you be asking to ride one first?'

Dunnkan smiled, 'Why, that would be me, of course.'

The royal guard were almost in arms protesting, but he waved them aside. Taking off his royal robe he was down at the field in moments. He and his guards stopped only a few paces away from Kialessa and her friends before entering.

'Not every day a king gets to be first, is it?' he whispered to them.

Allastassia almost opened her mouth as though she might try and talk him out of it, but instead kept silent.

'Be careful!' Piex fretted.

'Have fun!' Kialessa cheered.

The king winked at them all, and waited while the boards were removed for him to enter. Baroness Emerald showed him how to mount the horse and ride it safely, while two armed guards stood close by him in case there was any trouble. There wasn't, and soon he was safely mounted and grinning broadly while she led the horse in a circle.

'They ride well, beast master!' he called to the servant in charge of his stables, who would keep the horses. The servant was standing with his arms folded, and his eyebrows knit together.

'The beast master's not so pleased about this, is he?' Kialessa said.

'He knows posks,' Darrix explained. 'He won't want the responsibility of looking after these strange creatures as well.'

'They ride slow!' the beast master complained.

'Aha! If 'tis speed you wishing for, you must meet Mask - son of the prince of horses. Clear the field!' baroness Emerald replied. She helped the king dismount and tied up the four horses. Then she returned with one of the males; a huge horse with a coat of glossy ebony, including the deep purple markings within his mane and hooves. He pawed the earth excitedly while the crowd grew silent.

'Posks are fine beasts!' she shouted. 'But if it's speed you want …'

With a mighty scream, the horse leapt up on its back legs, its front legs pawing the air as if it were about to climb straight up. It let out a terrific cry which made everyone step back, and then it leapt forward. It raced across the ground, sending great clods of earth into the air behind it. It was faster than any posk by more than double, and it crossed the entire field in moments. She turned it roughly and it raced back towards the crowd, who jumped away from the fence. All except for Kialessa, Posk and Piex.

As it raced past them time seemed to slow down. Kialessa thought she could hear its powerful heartbeat thudding into the ground through its massive legs. She heard Posk gasp.

The baroness stopped the horse just an instant before it would have crashed through the fence, crushing people behind it.

Everyone cheered.

'This horse is already being a great champion of my people; his price alone over two thousand coins! Who will

     By Dr Joseph Ireland "Dr Joe"

bid me for this horse's reins!' baroness Emerald held the reins out towards the people.

But no one would bid against the king … none but Posk, the young half troll boy, who swung himself up under the fence and raced out onto the field.

'Wait, no!' Darrix said, seeing the danger and racing after him. Piex begun to cast a spell, arcane light gathering in his fingers, but Allastassia stopped him.

'It won't stop the horse,' she said, fear and concern in her eyes.

Piex nodded and they watched helplessly to see how events would unfold.

Posk ran right up to the horse and held up his hand. The horse, only an animal and still breathing heavily from its exhilarating run, was surprised and frightened by the gesture. It reared up, almost tipping the baroness from her saddle. She tried to hold him by the reins, but they slipped from her grasp as the frightened horse whinnied and reared up again, sharp hooves flailing towards the little half troll.

Posk looked surprised and stepped back. He wasn't afraid of animals but this beast was strange and frightened. It crouched as though it was about to leap towards him and trample him underfoot, when another boy jumped in the way, holding one hand high above his head and shouted, 'STOP!'

5 Posk and the horse

The stallion immediately stopped and stood back, tossing its head uncertainly.

Darrix took a step towards it and spoke calmly to it, holding out his hand, palms down towards its face. The horse took a few steps backwards, whinnying. The crowed fell silent. Slowly, then gently, it stood forwards and touched his hand with its snout.

Baroness Emerald snatched up the reins again and wheeled the horse around.

'Stupid boy!' she shouted at Posk, who looked confused and ashamed. 'This horse is a warrior, not a beast of burden! It did not know you weren't attacking

     By Dr Joseph Ireland "Dr Joe"

him.'

It was clear to Kialessa that the baroness was trying to make the most the situation or the king might not buy her horses. 'You see how much power they contain, yet I could keep these children safe. But you must know how to treat them and respect them too!'

She cast a puzzled look at Darrix, who was staring down at his hand as though he'd just touched something he couldn't explain.

The boys were hurried from the field and made to wait far from the horses. Posk immediately ran off into his forest. Kialessa felt sorry for him.

By the end of the afternoon the king had bought four horses; both males and two females. Allastassia's family bought the whitest female and another rich noble purchased the remaining horse. They were all to be kept at the king's stable outside the castle walls, and the king even hired two new stable hands to watch over them. They had a special diet of grains that the baroness had brought, and she soon taught the gardeners how to grow it. She confidently assured everyone that rye was just a good for humans to eat, though few were willing to try the bitter drink she made from them after their initial taste.

Over the next few weeks all anyone would talk about was the horses. Of the two stallions, the largest was called Mask. While baroness Emerald rode him with great confidence and skill, the king's guards who were assigned to ride him had far worse luck. Kialessa heard they were being thrown from his back at the rate of about one a day. Word got out that the King had made a bad purchase, and that Mask would only be good for breeding newer, more sensible, horses. And Posk had not been seen in weeks.

Darrix quickly developed a new hobby – watching the strange new beasts. It became an almost obsessive passion, and even though he was a gem merchant's son, he would volunteer almost daily to shovel in the stables just so he could be with them. Much to the stable hands' chagrin, the horses loved him and would nuzzle up to him whenever he worked.

Thus, Kialessa was sure, his father would be in despair that his son would ever amount to anything at all.

Of friends

It may be a lifetime before you realise, and I'm more than sixty, so I would know! But some of the most important, key events of my life, that have defined all I am and have become, didn't look like it at the time. They just looked like any other day.

– King Dunnkan, 313, cited in, The Year in Jail.

On the next Serrosday afternoon, with nothing else to do, Kialessa packed up a little lunch for herself and wandered out into the forest. It was a lovely, quiet place, where few people went because it was so overgrown. There were plenty of thin nettled pine trees, so that as the wind blew, it would sound like the trees were talking, and they probably were.

It seemed like years ago, but it was only last season

that she had lived with her parents at the inn half a day's ride toward the sea. When she had lived with them, there was never half a Serrosday to go out and walk around by herself. It was peaceful, and though she never did much thinking while she was out there, new ideas seemed to find her easily enough in the quiet of the forest.

She was having fun tossing little pebbles into a stream when she heard a rustling in the underbrush behind her, and a sudden scratching sound of claws on earth. She turned around just as a shadow leapt out of the bushes right at her.

With a scream, she fell to the ground and it sailed over her, just missing her with razor sharp claws. It fell with a mighty *kersplash* into the river.

Her heart was beating like thunder in her chest as she ran screaming into the woods. But she didn't want to be scared of the forest, so she turned around to see what had leapt at her.

It was a drake – a kind of lesser dragon without wings. Drakes were longer than two posks but more narrow, yet their claws and teeth just as sharp.

She did not know there were drakes in this forest. Perhaps it had wandered from some other place? Perhaps it had been driven out from its home? It seemed fairly young, and as she watched, it lost its footing on the wet rocks in the stream. With a roar, it went head over heels and hit its chin on a rock. A dizzy look came over it, and it fell headfirst into the water.

She could have let it drown; after all, it had tried to eat her. But she didn't think anything related to a dragon would hurt *her*. She rushed down to the river and grabbed it by the tail, dragging it out.

It was hard work, getting the large reptilian's head out of the water, but she did it. Somehow the poor creature had managed to hold its breath while knocked senseless.

But her feelings of pity did not last long. As soon as it gained consciousness it sniffed the air and turned in her direction, licking its lips.

She ducked away from the whipping claws as it stumbled around, and tried to stand up again and grab her.

'Hey! I just saved your life!' Kialessa screamed.

But the drake only roared. It was just an animal and not intelligent like a dragon was. *Why isn't this working out like the fairy tales say?*

She jumped behind a tree and screamed again. It was the only tactic she had. She knew the drake could outrun her in an instant and climb trees much faster than she. It scraped and scrambled through the underbrush, but there was no outrunning a drake.

So she screamed again.

The next thing she knew there was flash of motion from the trees as something leapt out and smashed right into the side of the drake, knocking it sideways.

Kialessa wanted to run. She knew it was her chance to run but a new thought held her back. What if the thing saving her got into trouble?

Hoping that her curiosity really *wouldn't* kill her, she peered around the bushes to see what was happening. There, thrashing around among the grass, was Posk, and he was griping onto the drake's dangerous jaws with his bare hands. They were wrestling, both with the look of fierce determination in their eyes.

'Posk?!' Kialessa shouted in surprise, relief and fear all at once.

'Mrgrumph!' he shouted back.

She almost cried with relief to see him. She hadn't seen him since the incident with the horses. She didn't think he'd gone far but couldn't believe how he'd managed to be so close at hand. It was impossibly good luck.

Kialessa watched as the pair of forest-born foes thrashed and writhed in the woods. They made little noise as the drake concentrated on freeing itself and Posk concentrated on keeping the razor-sharp jaws clamped shut.

Suddenly the drake found its feet and took off at a terrific speed into the forest, Posk still clinging to its neck.

For the next hour she did nothing but try to keep up, shouting encouragement to Posk that he didn't seem to need. The drake thrashed and twisted, trying to break free for all it was worth. Kialessa knew if Posk ever let go he

 By Dr Joseph Ireland "Dr Joe"

would be dead in a heartbeat.

She kept trying to get close enough to hit it with a rock. How she wished she had a bow, or at least her old sling she used to chase birds from the apple orchard! But the drake was too fast for her to get close, and as soon as she did it would run away again, dragging the half troll boy along with it. The desperate struggles of the drake were clearly wearying it.

She paused, suddenly aware of just how far they'd come, and how desperately lost in the forest she was. Then she felt afraid, like the whispers of dark tendrils steaming around her heart. It brought back the echoes of a bad dream. She tried to push them from her mind before she remembered the terrible, hopeless feelings, but still its whispers seemed to find her.

Give up, it implored temptingly, *he can handle himself, or he's dead already. This is your only chance to flee!*

But she knew that was a lie, *Run? To where? That drake will only find me again. No, I can't give up. If not for my sake, then at least for Posk's!*

She ran away into the forest again, chasing the sounds of the distant battle. She didn't give up, closing the distance between them, aware now of how much the training at college had strengthened her.

She found them a moment later, thrashing in the woods. Posk had both hands around its muzzle as it tried to rub him off again on the trees as it ran.

Posk suddenly reached out and grabbed a small tree, halting the drakes latest dash. With a cry of victory Kialessa charged. But the monster lashed out with impressive speed, its tail knocking the wind out of her as it took off again into the forest. It rounded a natural hill and there was a large thump as something alive collided with something solid. There was the snap of draconic jaws, and Posk cried out.

The forest fell silent. Kialessa could only hear her fevered breathing as she struggled to stand. If the drake had won, it was sure to come for her next. But even that terrifying thought was drowned out by her fear for her friend.

She waited breathlessly, and listened. With growing disappointment she felt through her feet the steady thump, thump of a four-legged drake. The thumping grew louder, and it burst into view and charged straight for her. Posk was nowhere to be seen.

She jumped to the ground as it leapt over her, but instead of cringing there she pulled her whip and lashed it around its leg. Using a trick she'd learnt the hard way from a senior student, rather than try to hold it back using her own strength, she wrapped the whip around a nearby tree and held on for dear life.

When the whip sprung taut the drake yelled out and there was a *pop* as though it might have twisted its ankle. It collapsed on the forest floor.

     By Dr Joseph Ireland "Dr Joe"

She was about to run for her life when, with a roar, Posk leapt over her head. His arm was severely scratched, but not bleeding. He leapt on to the agonised drake and clamped its jaws shut once more.

He pressed down on its head, and held it steady for another ten moments till, tired and sore, it stopped thrashing.

It had surrendered.

'Do we go now?' Kialessa asked.

Posk shook his head, then did something a little strange. Still holding the snout, he manoeuvred till he could stare it right in its eyes for at least ten moments more. Then, slowly, he removed his hands.

It lay there for a moment. When it stood up, its head was bowed. Then it sat at Posk's feet and did not move. It looked a bit like a lost puppy.

Posk bent down and patted it. He indicated to Kialessa to bring water and took a large and deliberate drink right in front of it. Then he poured it carefully on the drake's injured foot, and gave it a little to drink.

It whimpered, as though it was apologising. Posk took a vine, snapped it from the tree, and wrapped it around the drake's head.

'Posk!' he ordered, and sitting on its back, pulled it to its feet. It was a little unsteady, but it stood, and he was riding it.

'Posk!' he said to Kialessa, almost as if he was

surprised, but obviously pleased. 'Hraa!' he roared, and he and the drake raced off into the forest once more, now as allies. Kialessa had to climb a tree to see where they were going, and cheered with delight as Posk and the drake ran around in circles, crashing through the underbrush and leaping over obstacles with great strides.

Posk had just tamed a drake. She'd never heard of that happening before.

They rode around for a good half hour or more before Posk brought the now amicable creature back and allowed Kialessa to pat it. It felt just like a dragon. Its skin was forest green with brown markings that would disguise it well in a wood like this. Its eyes were catlike and deep green, and almost looked intelligent. It had a strong frill that ran from its head to its tail, and while the drake was thin, it was superbly muscular.

'I wonder where this little fellow came from?' Kialessa asked, glad that Posk had turned up just in time to save her. The drake was strong, but younger and smaller than the drawings she'd seen in the college. She wondered if there were other drakes out in the woods. Perhaps a whole family?

The drake bent its head, and Posk too looked around in concern. The drake indicated a direction with its nose, and Posk nodded.

Yet Kialessa had heard nothing, and she was usually good at hearing.

      By Dr Joseph Ireland "Dr Joe"

Stalking like cats, Posk and his drake slowly made their way towards whatever was disturbing them.

Kialessa followed silently. 'They don't teach you this at college,' she muttered. Posk apparently had quite a few skills they weren't aware of, like how to survive alone in a forest for days at a time, and how to tame drakes that were twice his size.

Soon they came across a clearing where a huge beast was grazing. Kialessa stared in surprise – it was a horse. Its saddle had fallen half onto the ground and the beast was ignoring it, but it was definitely Mask, the big stallion that King Dunnkan had bought.

'What's that doing here?' Kialessa whispered. 'Shouldn't it be back at the stables?'

The drake looked like it would have attacked, even though the horse could probably have crushed its head with one hoof, but Posk pulled it back.

'I think they'd like it if we returned him.' Kialessa said out loud, but Posk looked like he didn't understand. She pointed at the horse and indicated she was going to try to talk to it, but Posk looked concerned and pulled at her arm.

They were busy debating what they should do, without using words, when from across the field another horse burst, ridden by none other than Darrix.

'Ha! Mask! We found you first! C'mon, then. Back, you!'

Mask reared up threateningly, and Darrix's horse almost threw him off in her fright. Mask was about to gallop off into the forest when Posk, who must have realised what Darrix was trying to do, ran his drake out into the clearing and blocked off Mask's escape.

The drake hissed at the horse and shook its frill threateningly at it.

Mask stopped.

'Posk?' Darrix said in surprise.

'Hrmmm!' Posk shouted back, bowing his head and holding out his arm.

'What?' Darrix asked.

But Kialessa understood and translated from her hiding place, 'Just like on the first day you met the horse! Calm him! Be gentle!' she said, too wise to involve herself in confronting the enormous animals personally.

'Kia too?!' Darrix said, looking around.

Mask was pawing the ground and whinnying anxiously. Darrix quickly jumped off his horse, and began walking towards him, speaking softly. He held his hand out, and slowly walked towards an animal almost twice his height.

The drake was anxious too, clearly not sure whether to fight or flee from the horse. But Posk kept it still and silent. He pulled back to the edge of the forest.

As Darrix approached, the horse seemed to lose its tension and fear. It calmed down as Darrix touched it.

Speaking softly, Darrix resaddled it and managed to put the bit in his mouth once more.

'You can't imagine how glad I am that you're here right when I needed you,' Darrix said to her.

'Don't thank me. I was following Posk!'

Darrix put Kialessa on the other horse, but she was unsure how to ride it. Thankfully, it was one of the good ones, and seemed willing to do all the hard work itself.

'Mask broke out this morning. The beast master sent out just about everyone looking for him. I hear there's someone famous coming to Lenmer'el, and the king is anxious to make a good impression.'

'Who?' Kialessa asked.

'Tomin,' Darrix said, 'one of the High King's most powerful warriors. It's big news, not everyday someone that important comes all the way out to little Lenmer'el, is it.'

'I guess not.'

'I suppose we should be getting back then,'

'All right, which way?' Kialessa asked.

'I don't… I don't actually know.'

In the end, he decided to take an old riverbed in the hope it was the right way. Kialessa thought it foolish that they hadn't paid more attention in mapping and geography, realising she'd been relying on Piex's amazing memory to guide her all this time. Mask and the drake rode on the far sides of the dry river, eyeing each other cautiously, while Kialessa rode in the middle, constantly grateful she was riding one of the well trained and reliable horses. Even so, within an hour her backside was so sore it was numb, and she had to keep adjusting herself because this saddle wasn't built for people with tails.

Darrix stopped. 'It's getting late, and … I think we're lost.'

The sun was indeed getting low in the sky, and Kialessa was beginning to wonder herself if they knew where they were going. They carried on for another hour, but the sun had set, and there was no sign of the castle they called home.

'Let's find somewhere to settle for the night,' Darrix said.

Neither of them liked the idea of sleeping in the open woods, except perhaps Posk, who was showing no sign of being bothered in any way. She wondered if he slept out in the open every day, because when she tried to ask him to show her the way home he acted as though he either didn't know, or didn't understand what she was asking.

'Do you think King Dunnkan will miss his horses?' Kialessa asked.

'I was one of a dozen solders who went out to find Mask when he broke the field and ran this morning. I decided to join in because I'm one of the few who can ride a horse too. When I first found Mask, he'd been grazing on some hills and took off again. I lost the man who was

     By Dr Joseph Ireland "Dr Joe"

with me about then; he was riding a Posk. Posks don't like horses very much. I'd been chasing Mask for about three hours by the time you caught up to him, and I'm glad you did. He was just about to take off into the hills again.'

'Have you ever ridden him before?' Kialessa asked.

He smiled and reached forward to pat the enormous animal on the neck, his smile doing little to hide his concern, 'Never, and never has anyone ridden him this long. I don't know what has happened. But, in all honesty, I really wish I knew where we were going, or a lost animal may end up being the least of our concerns…'

A good day

*What compares with the glory of battle and the death of
your enemies! A nice warm bed and cup of hot cocoa.
– 9th Saying of the irrefutable sage of Venterrin.*

The sun was gone, and evening began to fill the
woods. Soon mist rose up from the ground, as it usually
did, and Kialessa feared they would soon be lost for good.
'We'd better find somewhere to stay the night.'

'Posk seems to know where he's heading,' Darrix
replied.

Indeed he did. They'd been riding side by side,
chatting to pass the time. But Posk and his drake were
skirting on ahead. They would wait for them to catch up,
then burst off along the trail again. Even though the drake

          By Dr Joseph Ireland "Dr Joe"

was much faster than a horse, it could only keep it up for a short time. But the pace seemed to suit Posk nicely, and he even found time to hunt a few rabbits which he tied to his belt. He fed them intermittently to his mount.

'They seem to be getting along quite well. How long has he ridden a drake?' Darrix asked.

'Since this morning. It tried to eat me.'

'Really? You mean, he tamed a drake this morning?' Darrix sounded bemused.

'I believe so. Singlehandedly clamped its jaws shut for over an hour. They seem to be loyal beasts, once they're tamed.'

'That they do.' Darrix sat thinking for a moment. Then, without speaking his thoughts, he patted Mask on the neck and the horse whinnied in reply.

At Posk's insistence, they headed up a hill on an old trail that was well made but didn't seem to be used anymore. As the sky grew dark enough to make Darrix complain about it, they saw a little wooden shack with a light in the window.

They were both glad to see the warm glow inside and another horse tied up in the open stable. They made their way to the small building and tied their horses next to it under the wide, overhanging roof.

Posk muttered seriously to his drake for a moment, then set it free into the woods.

'Don't worry, you'll see him aga–' Kialessa began.

'MWA ROOO!' Posk suddenly bellowed, and in a moment, the drake came bursting back through the trees. Posk laughed, patted it, and fed it a rabbit whole.

'See, told you so.' Kialessa said, even though she knew Posk had done it all himself. He was training the drake to come when he called. Just to be sure, he repeated it twice more.

'You don't suppose it'll attack the horses, do you?' Kialessa asked.

'Not with Mask there,' Darrix replied. 'Very little in these woods would risk that. Except a pack of wolves, and we'd hear them.'

'Darrix!' a voice called from the doorway of the little shack. It was Allastassia.

'What is this, some kind of reunion!?' Kialessa said with a grin.

'Allastassia!' Darrix said, and returned her hug. 'Look, Kialessa and Posk are here too. But what are you doing out here in the woods?'

'Oh!' Allastassia huffed. 'Those stupid horses. When mother heard that you'd gone out on *my family's* horse –'

'Oh, is this your family horse?' Kialessa asked. 'She's very nice.'

'Yes, quite. Well, when mother heard, she sent out dozens of messengers to make sure my horse didn't get lost. So she's got me out here with my barely conscious uncle who does nothing but sleep all day, just in case any messengers pass by here, and what do you know! Now Posk is shouting about who knows what.'

'He's calling his drake,' Kialessa explained.

'His what?'

'His drake. He has a pet drake,' Darrix replied.

'Not really a pet. More of a tamed … companion I think.' Kialessa thought out loud. 'I don't think they've met before today.'

'No one can tame a drake!' Allastassia said.

'Posk can.' Kialessa smiled.

As they watched, out on a nearby hill and neatly silhouetted by the early evening moon, the half troll boy summoned his reptilian drake for one last time. It did not feed, but rather allowed him to hold its neck in a gentle embrace, while it twisted its head around to rest against his shoulders. As the wondrous moment drew to its silent end, the powerful drake scampered away into the night to await its companion's call in the morning.

Allastassia was speechless.

'No one, except Posk.' Darrix repeated.

6 Posk and the drake

'Well … whatever.' Allastassia said dismissively, but Kialessa could tell she was impressed. 'Now we're here. I suppose we'll need to let the others know you're all right and you've got the horses and we're going to bring them back in the morning. No point heading out now with all the night creatures out.'

'How we going to let them know all that?' Kialessa asked.

'This'll do the trick,' Allastassia said, and using a wand, shot five blue balls of pure light that burned high into the night sky. 'One for each of us,' she explained, 'and blue to say we've found the horses and will bring them back tomorrow. Maybe they'll even send in some food. Did you guys bring any?'

'No,' Darrix said, 'I took off after Mask with nothing but the clothes I had on. I'm actually quite hungry.'

'You're always hungry,' Allastassia told him, laying a hand on his arm.

'True, true.'

'I did bring a picnic, but we've finished all that,' Kialessa said. 'Do you like cooked rabbit?'

She wrinkled her nose at that. Kialessa wasn't surprised. Allastassia had eaten at the tables of kings and was probably used to duck or even baked ferrenwosk.

'We'll just have to see what other things my *dumb* uncle brought,' Allastassia said.

He was truly the sleepiest man Kialessa had ever met and could barely lift an arm without being ordered to. They were left to prepare for sleep while the uncle rested his head on his arm, one eye half open to keep an eye on them all, or at least to pretend he did.

Posk, much to Allastassia's discomfort, wanted to sleep indoors with the rest of them. With a bed for the enchantress, a couch for Darrix, and the table to support her uncle where he lay, there was no other bedding for anyone else.

'There's got to be some straw around,' Kialessa said.

'What?' Darrix argued, 'No, Kialessa, you're *not* sleeping on straw. It's undignified.'

'I don't mind.'

'No, you take the couch. I'm –'

Suddenly there was a *whoosh*, and in teleported a small boy laden with blankets and pillows and jars of preserved food. She couldn't see his face over the bundles he was carrying.

'The noble wizard Coeur De'Feur bids you all good rest in the cabin and thanks all involved for the rescue of the king's valued … hey, it's **you** folks!'

It was Piex.

'See!' Kialessa grinned, 'It *is* a reunion!'

'What're you doing here?' Allastassia inquired.

'Sagemaster De'Feur teleported me here to help whoever rescued the king's horses and make sure they were properly fed. It's you folks. I can't believe it's you folks! What're you folks doing out here?'

'Losing a bit of your natural flair with language are you, Piex?' Allastassia teased.

'Oh, forgive me,' he said, 'but the mutual acceptation of your presence at this serendipitous location has caused unforeseen elation, which renders my usual perspicacity inoperable at this time.'

They laughed as they helped themselves to the bounty of food and bedding. It was enough for five grown humans, so there was more than enough for all of them and one sleepy uncle. Kialessa wished the wizard could simply teleport them all back, but there were probably good reasons why he didn't work such grand magic for such trivial things, and one simply didn't ask great

     By Dr Joseph Ireland "Dr Joe"

wizards their reasons.

The fire cheered them and Allastassia's family cabin was now well stocked for surprise visitors lost in the woods. They all heard about Posk's heroic defeat of the drake and how he'd saved Kialessa, and how Darrix had calmed the king's prize horse and ridden it for the first time today. Then they watched as Piex and Allastassia competed to make the most impressive bird illusions, complete with beautiful warbling bird songs. It was a magical evening, one that none of them wanted to end.

But eventually Allastassia's uncle Joesef informed them it was late enough, and insisted they continue talking with their heads on pillows while he plucked softly on his lute. Kialessa made a comfortable nest out of straw and blankets, and Allastassia unconsciously covered her bed with flower petals. Posk slept on the floor in a ball, but Piex ended up sleeping next to him for warmth. Darrix moved the couch by the windows just so that could hear the tinkling of the nearby stream, claiming it helped him relax. Then they settled down to listen to the strumming of the lute. It seemed to be magic too, for within moments they were all asleep.

****

By dawn, the sleepy uncle had managed to fill a tub with water and insisted they wash their faces and arms before they started out, though they were not half a day from the castle. Eventually, Posk's drake arrived for feeding and friendship, and Darrix wondered out loud how they'd travel back.

'I have that covered.' Allastassia said, and placing a small, ivory figurine of a horse into the ground, magic twingled around her. 'This is a new one, Piex,' she boasted, sweat breaking out on her brow. An invisible breeze whipped around her clothes and hair, as it often did when she was working her magic, and her hands glowed a rich blue light. Vivid purple lightning sparked down into the ground.

'Is the lightning really necessary?' Piex complained.

'I'm still getting the hang of this one,' Allastassia replied, concentrating hard. 'It's one my mother taught me ... much better at it ...'

The ground in front of her bulged slightly, then leapt up to form a massive mound in front of the enchantress. Within moments, a strange creature begun to shake the dirt from its back. It was wide and powerful, and had pure white fur. It had four limbs, dangerous tusks, and the deepest magical blue eyes Kialessa had ever seen.

'It's a –' Kialessa began.

'Whentiki's marvellous mage mount,' Piex ensaged.

'A Posk!' Allastassia said triumphantly, but looked a little tired.

'But you don't conjure them from the ground,' Piex

          By Dr Joseph Ireland "Dr Joe"

said, 'It's not a summoning spell, you –'

'It's a posk,' Allastassia said, the sound of elation gone from her voice.

'I've seen Master Coeur De'Feur do this spell,' Piex went on, 'but his mount is deep blue. It's –'

'A POSK!' Allastassia suddenly shrieked. 'I was *trying* for a horse! Why is it a stupid POSK?'

She hit it with her hand, but it didn't even budge as though it was a statue or something.

Wisely, perhaps, Piex fell silent.

'Didn't work out the way you expected, Alli?' Darrix teased with a disarming grin.

'Oh, I do this all the time,' she replied.

He smiled. 'This is the first time you've ever done this enchantment, isn't it?'

'I … well … yes,' she admitted. She had clearly wanted to impress them all, 'But why is it a posk? I *hate* posks. Horses are much more impressive.'

'You could have tried a drake?' Kialessa said, not understanding what was wrong with a posk. Allastassia had created a creature to carry her using nothing but an enchanted pewter figurine and her imagination. What did it matter what it looked like?

'Stupid posks,' Allastassia muttered, but got up anyway.

As it was, Mask would let no one other than Darrix ride him, so in the end Kialessa rode with Allastassia's horse, Posk on the drake, and Uncle Joesef rode with Piex on the other horse. Allastassia rode sullenly on her magical mount, which glistened beautifully and looked just as gorgeous as she did in the morning sun.

And that was how they rode into town, everyone stopping their work and downing tools to watch them, pointing at them in amazement as they rode past. The King was overjoyed and rewarded them handsomely for restoring his horse. Kialessa was just happy with his hugs, but Allastassia made a speech out of it. Once more, they were the toast of the town for that week, though few people dared to believe that Posk had tamed a real live drake until they saw him riding it, which he did every day from then on.

Kialessa never forgot that day. It was a good day.

     By Dr Joseph Ireland "Dr Joe"

The paladin

Religious feelings are strong among our people and religion is a very real thing in our world. I believe we should talk about it, at least occasionally.

– Humdug, dwarf scholar.

There had been rumours about it for weeks, though Kialessa never really paid much attention because she did not know what a paladin was. But the day he arrived, as Kialessa readied her hair in the dormitory before the sun was even up, everyone was talking about him, so there wasn't anyone to tell.

'Oh, we've known since last year,' Allastassia boasted. 'He's going to bless a new sword father had forged while he's here.'

'Will he be staying at your estate?' Patsi asked.

'No, I hear the king offered him his royal suite, but Tomin, that's his name, paladin of Serros, insists on staying in the servants' quarters because he doesn't deem himself worthy. Almost makes me wish **I** was a servant!' She giggled with the rest of the girls in the dormitory.

Later that day, Allastassia was reading to Kialessa during Historical studies when the sound of trumpets went up from the walls, announcing his arrival. They rushed to the windows and pressed their noses to the cool, wrinkled glass, hoping to catch a glimpse of the famous warrior.

'Keep reading your history texts!' the tutor insisted, and they all sighed in disappointment.

'But sir, we're *making* history!' Allastassia argued.

'Well, I don't suppose it will hurt to take a moment out of class to see history in the *making*,' he smiled.

Tutors never seem to mind when she argues with them, Kialessa thought.

But she noticed the tutor grinning to himself. Maybe he wanted to see history too. With a multitude of further instructions, he herded them outside and down to the main street of the castle to join the many citizens. They lined the street in excited throngs as the visitor came into view.

The paladin was an amazing sight. He was tall, well built and, yes, quite handsome for an older human male. But it was difficult to tell details under the layers of solid metal he wore. Both his shield and banner bore his emblem of a wreath of silver leaves on a blue background; after all, he was from one of the northern fiefdoms of Nomer'el.

His banner was pinned to the end of his huge lance and a glistening shield hung from his saddle, both bearing the scars of many battles, including the three dragons he was famous for having slain. He rode a great grey Posk that was almost as tall as the horses.

'What makes him different from other soldiers?' Kialessa asked.

'What?' Piex said. 'He's a **paladin**. They're not only warriors but also like priests, wielding great power of the gods. They are sworn to solemn oaths of purity and fidelity that grant them great faculty. They are some of the most powerful and inspiring warriors of the High King's army.'

'And most handsome!' Allastassia gushed.

Well, thought Kialessa, *he is fairly handsome, for a human.*

'That's not what they're about,' Darrix disagreed.

'What?' Kialessa asked.

He turned, looking serious. 'Paladins are about showing that the highest standards **can** be kept and **are** rewarded. They're not about being strong or holding oaths, or even looking handsome.'

'Oh,' Allastassia said, sounding like he'd taken the

wind out of her sails.

By now Tomin, paladin of Serros, was approaching them while everyone waved. Allastassia caught his eye, as she often did, and he smiled brightly at her. But when he came to Kialessa, he stopped sharply and looked down in surprise.

Kialessa wondered how perfect his control over his mount must be for it to know exactly when and how he wanted to stop like that. She didn't like the look in those piercing, deep brown eyes. There was surprise and … danger.

There was an uncomfortable silence between Kialessa and the paladin while they stared at each other, and the noise of the cheering crowds seemed to drift away. Then Allastassia did something Kialessa never thought she'd do – she put her arm around and hugged her, all the time waving in the friendliest manner at the glowering paladin.

An instant later he moved on, looking down at them with a puzzled expression on his face.

'I don't think he likes me,' Kialessa admitted.

'Never mind that,' Allastassia replied. 'Come, let's see what happens when he meets the king!'

But they weren't allowed in when he was meeting the king for the first time, though Kialessa guessed there would be a lot of bowing and graceful, well-chosen words. They weren't allowed to see how the great paladin trained the guards, or when he unleashed his holy might on the king's elite and they were sorely tested by his strength. They weren't even allowed to see the king's chapel that evening to hear the paladin give a sermon on purity and valour. But they heard all about it though – it was all anyone was talking about.

But it was all words, and words were as close as Kialessa expected to get to the paladin during his stay. So it was no small surprise when, on the afternoon of his third day, the great Tomin, paladin of Serros, turned up to college training.

The athletics master was eager to show off his most talented students, so it was only natural that he put Kialessa and her closest friends through some of their toughest tests ever. Together they faced an illusionary dungeon filled with spectral shadows, and, once more, they defeated the entire group of senior students at capture the flag. Allastassia impressed them all with a new fan of lightning spell, and Kialessa made it all the way through the dancing ropes test, the youngest ever to do so.

But what the paladin thought of this Kialessa did not know. He simply looked and said nothing. But he stopped to speak once he saw Darrix training.

'You are well trained for one so young,' he said as soon as Darrix and the older boy he was with stopped sparring.

'Thank you, Honoured,' Darrix bowed.

The paladin smiled. 'And gracious too. Good qualities, indeed. Would you wish to train with me?'

'I would!' Darrix replied, even before the words had finished leaving Tomin's mouth. It made the paladin laugh. All the activities in the room ground to a sudden halt so people could watch.

'Very well, but I see you are trained as one of the senior students now, so we will be training in steel, not wooden swords.'

Kialessa could hear several students' gasp.

'Don't worry, I won't hurt him too much!' The paladin laughed, as did many others, as if on cue. He seemed to laugh a lot.

'Here boy, you have a warrior's build. I will allow you an advantage I don't usually offer to students I train with,' he pulled a sword from his belt. It was bright, almost glowing, and had the words of sacred prayer inscribed along its gilded blade.

'This sword I have named Defender. His power can be used for attack or defence, and not all swords have such a talent.'

'I've heard of that,' Piex said, trying to be helpful. Everyone looked at him, but no one said anything.

The sword initially seemed just a little large for Darrix, but then it appeared to shrink to the perfect size. Darrix swung it with a grin.

'Well, stand back all, we've training to attend to,' the

paladin announced.

The other students, the two professional soldiers and Kialessa all stood back to let Darrix and the paladin spar. Kialessa was nervous, as they were live blades. Blood was inevitable, death… anxiously close.

'Remember, flat of the sword only,' Tomin reminded him, and Darrix nodded.

They circled for a bit before Darrix struck. Tomin didn't even flinch. He blocked Darrix's sword and brought his own down towards the boy's head. It would have struck, but Darrix dodged nimbly out of the way.

'Methinks you have already seen the true peril of battle,' Tomin said.

'Yes,' Darrix replied, without boasting.

They fought a few more moments and Darrix took many blows, falling to the ground twice. But he got up again every time he fell, even though he fell quite hard both times.

'You've a warrior's spirit, that is certain!' the paladin said. 'Perhaps you might become a paladin of Serros yourself one day?'

The tutor looked surprised, and even Kialessa knew it was just about the highest compliment Tomin could have paid Darrix.

So Darrix's reply was a surprise to everyone. 'I do not take after the old gods, Honoured,' he replied, still circling and looking for his chance.

Tomin stood back, looking surprised. Darrix saw his opening and struck, but Tomin was too fast and parried his blows with ease, sending the young boy struggling out onto the ground once more.

'The old Pantheon is to be revered by all. It is the edict of the High King,' Tomin stated, sounding almost puzzled.

'I know,' Darrix said, standing. 'But my faith, my light, is from the Eternal.'

Tomin looked displeased and began to look down on the young man who struggled against him. 'You'll find no power beyond the law, young man. It is your shield and your sword. Move beyond its bounds and you lose its protection. Make up your own law and you lose its strength to fight injustice.'

Darrix pondered this, even as he traded blows with the seasoned paladin. 'I keep every law I am given and have done so from my childhood. I honour the old Pantheon on the required days. But I must be honest with you, Honoured. I am of the Eternal.'

Tomin smiled. 'This honesty is good. But your faith is surely misplaced. This … Eternal, this new god. Does he grant you prayers of power?'

'He does. Through me he has healed –'

'Then show me this faith!' Tomin challenged with a cunning grin.

Darrix paused, then stood up to his full height.

Kialessa knew what was happening. He was praying a warrior's prayer. This was not a simple training match for him anymore – it was a chance to convince others of the power and reality of his god. This meant **everything** to Darrix. For this chance, he would gladly take on a warrior four times his age and ten times his skill. For this, he would willingly die.

'By the Eternal!' Darrix shouted, and the white flames leapt upon his sword. A few of the senior students stood back – they knew when this happened, they would lose. But what would happen to the famous paladin of Serros?

The battle changed, with Tomin forced to use a greater measure of his strength and skill. Darrix seemed as strong as a full-grown adult, equal to Tomin, though the paladin still outmatched him for skill. The holy sword 'defender' must have helped, but even so, it was unlike any battle they'd seen in some time.

Eventually Tomin stood back to catch his breath. 'You've some good faith, boy. You'd make a fine paladin of Serros one day,' he repeated.

'No. Thank you,' Darrix replied, though he was probably thinking something more blunt.

The paladin sighed. 'Yours is not the only god that can hear prayers, child. The High Kingdom is changing, the old ways are being restored. It would be wise to choose to honour an Elder god, and not one that is just newly named. Allow me to show you – Serros, *be my light*!' he shouted.

Bright yellow fire leapt on Tomin's sword, and Darrix's advantage was lost as the older paladin brought down a similar prayer, and doubled his own strength. They traded blows almost too fast to see, but Darrix was at no advantage to the seasoned, practiced hero, and did not fare well.

Suddenly Darrix performed a successful feint and struck Tomin, landing a solid blow squarely across his sword arm. In the same swift motion Tomin lifted his shield and smashed it right into Darrix's face, sending him sprawling to the ground. Tomin thrust the point of his sword out till it rested just above Darrix's chest. They both paused, and as the battle closed, the effect of their prayers faded.

The older paladin breathed heavily. 'Do you know what you did wrong?'

'I opted for a wounding blow instead of a killing one.'

'Good. You're clever, especially for a warrior, even more so for a paladin. But you've some *faith*, boy. You would be a great influence for good if you served the *true* gods –'

At that, Kialessa felt incensed. Perhaps it was seeing her friend hit so hard by a seasoned warrior right in the face, or perhaps she was just angry that he'd suggested that hers was in some way an 'untrue god'. But before she'd thought of it she shouted, 'I thought they were the

     By Dr Joseph Ireland "Dr Joe"

old gods.'

People gasped.

The paladin looked at her, a cold stare of uncertainty and danger in his eyes. When he spoke again, it was to Darrix, and that just made her angrier – he *still* refused to speak to her. 'If you served the Pantheon, you would be a great influence for good.'

7 The humbling

Darrix didn't move. 'The Eternal is my God,' he repeated quietly, without arrogance.

Tomin stood back and spoke loudly. 'I want you *all* to know this. The law is your sword and your shield. Go against it and you will know only suffering. The High King has ordered all to worship the Elder gods of the old Pantheon, and this is the rightful law. Even the *Eternal* knows this. You do not break the law – you only break yourself against it.'

With that, he walked out.

Many students and tutors went with him, all of them muttering their own thoughts. One or two made sure their thoughts were loud enough to be heard, negative thoughts about an obnoxious new god and the arrogant young merchant's son who upset the great Tomin by insisting on believing in Him.

Darrix's closest friends gathered around him after the tutor had silently, but compassionately, taken the sword 'Defender' with him. Darrix did not try to hide the tears that welled up in his eyes.

'Hey, you've taken worse hits that that,' Allastassia tried to cheer things up.

Posk patted him on the head.

'Thanks, guys,' Darrix said. 'But I think I may have dishonoured my god instead of bringing praise to Him.' He said with tears in his eyes and looked at Kialessa, the only person he knew who would understand just *how much* that hurts.

    By Dr Joseph Ireland "Dr Joe"

Whispers

A sword will change the world, it is true.
But a prayer is just as effective, in my experience!
– Tomin, paladin of Serros.

Kialessa didn't like that paladin, though he was known as a warrior of might and virtue and goodness. It wasn't his unkind treatment of Darrix or even the dangerous, silent way he looked at her. It was the way he spoke of her religion.

She was not supposed to be worried; she was supposed to forgive her enemies and give kindness to those who treated her spitefully. But she didn't like that paladin!

So when Darrix was summoned out of dinner that evening, she slipped away as well. She knew who'd be calling.

The paladin.

It was obvious to her now that Tomin had come at the High King's order to straighten out the rebellious King Dunnkan and force the "official beliefs" of the old gods on the people. It wasn't fair how the High King was telling them all what to think and believe. And it wasn't normal; it hadn't happened in living memory.

But that was what the paladin was doing. And if Darrix didn't think the way the paladin wanted him to, he might influence people to believe in a god Tomin didn't like. To the famous warrior that would be, no doubt, insufferable.

So as silent as the nighttime that surrounded them, she slipped out into the darkness and followed Darrix through the castle.

Sure enough, the mighty paladin Tomin was waiting for him in the covered stone entryway between the lower castle and training grounds. Kialessa took a little while to run around to the other side, where she could hear them best, and was not surprised to hear that Tomin was whispering already. She climbed up the outside wall and let herself into the domed arched roof in the entryway. It was pitch black and the sounds echoed off the roof perfectly so that even whispers were easy to hear.

'… the employ of your father?' Tomin was asking.

'No,' Darrix replied. 'I don't take to that either, and he

finds me rebellious at the thought too, Honoured. He is a merchant of mining – gems and precious stones.'

'I see,' Tomin stated, revealing nothing of his thoughts.

Kialessa slipped into the domed roof at this point and Darrix caught sight of her just above Tomin's head. Thankfully, he said nothing.

'And what of the company you keep, boy? What of the fair dryad that is your age?'

'She'd nice, I suppose.'

'She is very fair.'

'She is.'

Tomin paused, as though he was looking for something more.

'And,' he asked eventually, 'what of the other company you keep, the tae'anaryn?'

'She is one of my truest friends.'

Tomin spoke in a voice gentle with respect. 'You must beware the company you keep, boy, to never be willingly in the company of evil lest they corrupt you.'

'Then you have nothing to fear of the tae'anaryn Kialessa,' Darrix replied.

Tomin paused again, as if searching for more. 'I will trust your word, young man, for it must be worthy of my trust. But be wary, for I have met many tae'anaryl in my day, and **all** have earned the end of my blade. But if you will speak for her, then I will trust her too, till her actions convince me otherwise …'

*So that **is** it*, Kialessa thought. *He really **does** hate tae'anaryl. It* made Kialessa angry, but then she wondered if all tae'anaryl really were so vile as to earn death at this paladin's hand?

And why?

'But I suppose you are wondering why I have called you here?' Tomin asked.

'Yes, Honoured,' Darrix replied, voice polite.

'Well,' he sounded uncomfortable, 'it is this. I have said more than I intended to today, but all I have said is true. Young boy, this is a great burden to place upon such young shoulders, but my heart tells me that this news is for you. You must promise me that you will not tell any, until the time is right.'

Darrix looked right into the paladin's eyes. 'I solemnly state that **I** will never tell anyone your news, till it is clear to me that such a time is right.'

Kialessa smiled. **He** promised not to tell. But the paladin hadn't asked if **he** was the only one listening.

'Does your god not ask for oaths?' the paladin queried.

'The Eternal asks us to make no oaths, only let our yes be yes and our no be no, and that is all that should be.'

Tomin pondered. 'He asks for honesty, even if He cannot bind His own people … but your word is enough for me, young man. The news is this – as a warrior in great honour in the High King's court I am privilege to much information, many of which sickens me with the wickedness and impurity of the world in which we live. But sometimes news arrives which truly appals me to the **bone** …'

Darrix waited in silence, as did Kialessa. When Tomin spoke, it was very quietly, 'War is coming.'

There is one rule when listening to others who do not know you listen, and that is to keep silence; no coughing, no laughing. No gasps of fear and surprise. Kialessa struggled to keep this rule.

So it was true.

'Pray it is not so,' Darrix said.

'It is so, but war is still a way off, methinks. A few seasons, I believe, but not many. It is hard to say and I am doing all I can to fight against it. But this foe is elusive, dangerous … almost, **poisonous**. It is not like other enemies which I have fought and which the High King has fought against for many years. I do not know what this means for the kingdom, but I, from the core of my being, believe the High King's edict to honour the old Pantheon is truly in the best interests of the people and of their children.'

Darrix was silent.

Kialessa had a thousand questions but couldn't ask any of them. She silently hoped somehow Darrix would know what to say. *Just keep him talking! Get him to drop another clue!*

'War?' Darrix asked.

'Indeed, unlike any … yet exactly like every war our people have ever fought.'

'Do you think the Great Kingdom will stand?'

'Of course!' Tomin replied without hesitation, 'though there may be many sacrifices. Oh, that we could snuff this wickedness out while it was still a spark, we would never have to battle the flames! This adversary, this foe, is not like other foes! But we **will** prevail, especially united. Especially united under the true gods of the Old pantheon.'

Darrix thought for a moment, 'An enemy unlike others? Perhaps a new weapon is needed?'

'And it is for such a weapon I seek, and new talent for the High King's army. As well as news we can use against this enemy.'

'Perhaps the weapon you seek is the very Eternal you disregard?' Darrix suggested.

The paladin laughed in good humour. 'If it is, I will embrace him in a moment! But it is not and only united faith in what has supported us for centuries can protect us.'

Darrix was silent.

'I have you told the words of my heart, words that I believe Serros would have me to teach to you tonight, to illuminate your mind and lead you to a stronger faith in his light. Go well, boy, and respect your father.'

'I will, Honoured,' Darrix said, 'and may you never know fear.'

Tomin laughed out loud. 'It is the gift of a paladin of Serros to never know fear!' With that, he left, sharp steel-clad boots striking the damp stones of the castle.

Darrix waited two moments and walked out onto the field before speaking to her.

She swung down.

'What do you think?' he asked.

'War is coming,' she repeated.

'And the first war will be against the Eternal,' Darrix predicted.

Kialessa was silent.

The rebellion of King Dunnkan

'Living forever isn't hard,' the goddess explained. 'Living forever with your choices can be almost impossible.'

'Then how are any to find peace?' the Emperor implored.

'Always stand up for what you believe, and be kind to yourself when you do not.'

– A conversation reportedly between the Dragon Emperor of Civit Aurea and Animas, goddess of the hunt. Origin unknown.

The early summer rain was falling heavily by the time

the next messenger from the High King arrived, two weeks later. It was a pompous noble this time, flanked by two important looking scholars who took down every word she said and cast serious and sober looks at everyone they met. She insisted on staying in the royal suite and didn't leave for two days. After that, everywhere she went she carried a great bronze disk emblazoned with the new symbol for the old Pantheon. It didn't take her long to leave a copy at the largest smithy in the town.

Darrix's father was livid. 'I built almost two hundred medallions of the old Pantheon, and now they go and change the design on me!'

Kialessa and Darrix were looking down at the disk the second messenger had provided for Darrix's father to copy. Several skilled craftsmen were already getting to work on building stamps and moulds of the disk for future work. A master craftsman was preparing a huge, almost adult sized copy for display in public places and the homes of the devout or especially rich.

'This symbol to Serros looks wrong,' Darrix said. 'It is as if it is eclipsed by this mountain motif.'

'Why is that?' Kialessa asked.

'Oh, some new artist's interpretation of the divine,' Darrix's father huffed. 'As long as it's on the medallion, it's going on every future one that this workshop produces!'

'But why change the symbol of Serros? Are we sure it's the same god now?' Darrix asked.

'Of course it is! See, this is clearly a sun motif, with the rays and everything. Don't worry about it, son.'

But, Kialessa thought, *it is a different symbol …*

The rest of the workshop was too busy to be bothered that afternoon, so Darrix and Kialessa left.

It was Planasday again, and Darrix had suggested that the five friends go out for a ride. Kialessa and Darrix turned up at the gate first, and while it took him fifteen moments of gentle convincing, Mask eventually allowed Kialessa to ride behind Darrix. It was exciting to be so high up on a horse, but still not as much fun as riding a dragon.

Posk arrived next, scampering in on his drake. He was usually found in this area of the woods, and Kialessa was glad to see they were not disappointed.

Piex was next. He was carrying a broom.

'What's that for?' Kialessa asked. She wondered what he was planning to clean up.

'I'm going to ride it with you,' he said, with a glum frown.

'Is it a magic broom?' Darrix said.

'Yes.' Piex pouted.

'What's a magic broom?' Kialessa asked.

'It can fly,' Darrix explained.

'Why make a broom fly? Sounds uncomfortable.'

     By Dr Joseph Ireland "Dr Joe"

Again, Piex sighed sadly. 'Oh, there are wizardly reasons.'

'Are you going to fly on it?'

Piex just sighed and didn't look up.

'Oh go on then, what's the matter?' Darrix asked.

'Well, Master heard we were all going out for a ride and grabbed this thing out of his closet. Told me he's had it all the time. I've never seen him ride it. He seems to think I'd know how.'

'It can't be that hard. It's magic,' Kialessa said.

'Actually, it is. While the broom might manage thrust, I'm still not certain how to manage the pitch and yaw, and assume bodily movements are required,' Piex said.

'You'll manage.' Darrix said, looking like he was trying to be helpful, but not looking very confident about it.

Sighing, Piex straddled the broom and sat down gently. He floated in mid-air.

In spite herself, Kialessa gasped. 'That's great, Piex. Look, you're flying!'

'I don't like flying,' he said, wobbling unsteadily on the broom.

'Does it go forwards?' Darrix asked.

'I think so … forwards?' Piex told the broom, and ever so slowly, it inched forwards, Piex wobbled every step of the way.

Slowly it began to climb and he, in a series of panicked

shouts, commanded it back down again. Eventually, he almost fell off, and he stopped it and got off with a snarl of disgust. 'That's awful. I think it's broken.'

'It's not broken,' Allastassia said. They had been so busy watching Piex they hadn't noticed her arrive. 'It's just that you're too worried. It's trying to do exactly what you tell it to and you're telling it that it's unstable and you're frightened. So stop worrying and fly straight.'

'Have you ridden one before!?' Piex said.

'Oh, my uncle's wife has one,' Allastassia replied. 'We take it for a spin every time we're at Sanmer'el. He doesn't let me go above the trees but it's quite simple once you stop worrying about it and let the broom do the flying.'

Piex was silent.

'Here, I'll show you.' She snatched the broom from his outstretched hand. He almost seemed glad to let it go.

In less than an instant she was up, making great graceful sweeps of beautiful curves and rapid dives. When she set it down again, she didn't boast, but gave Piex a happy look that was almost contagious. 'See, Piex, it's really fun. You're a wizard. You can do it.'

He mumbled something that they couldn't hear and probably weren't supposed to, but he got back on the broom and started out. He was a little shaky at first, but the ride slowly became smoother and smoother. However, he never went so high that he could not touch the ground with at least one foot.

'Gee,' muttered Darrix, 'he gets to borrow a flying broom and refuses to go any higher than he could walk.'

'I'm ready, then.' Piex announced, as if that meant they'd all be leaving now.

'Will you be riding with Posk?' Darrix teased Allastassia, who had arrived on foot. Since her last attempt Allastassia had refused to recast her mount enchantment. But now she huffed indignantly and created her magical mount once more. Once again, it was a beautiful white Posk with crystal blue eyes.

She got up without a word.

'And what about you, Kialessa?' Allastassia asked. 'We need to get you a ride.'

'She has one,' Piex called from the front, where he looked like he was struggling to turn the broom around.

She'd hoped he wouldn't bring that up. Kialessa did have a "ride". But she wasn't sure if riding on the back of one of your friends counted … and she didn't mean Posk. Kialessa had not heard from the young dragon, Eclipse, since they'd left the wizard Tobiuus' tower at summer's dawn. Perhaps Eclipse was sleeping like she'd said? Or perhaps causing trouble for her beautiful and kind mother wherever such creatures lived? Kialessa would have loved to have flown in the clouds with Eclipse again, but she didn't know if it was proper to say that she "rode" a dragon or if it was more correct to say that the dragon "took" her.

'What mount?' Darrix asked, 'a posk or a horse?'

'A dragon!' Piex replied for her, stopping the broom and turning it around by hopping along the ground. He didn't even look up, so he couldn't see the look of worry on Kialessa's face. She had wanted to keep that a secret.

Darrix and Allastassia were curious, and even Posk joined in their oohs and aahs, though he probably had no idea what was so exciting as they trundled along the road.

'I didn't know you rode a dragon!' Allastassia said.

'I don't know if you can say I *rode* her, but yes, she is my friend. A dragon called Eclipse. I don't know where she is now. We were supposed to learn to ride dragons at Tobiuus' tower. One of the "privileges", I suppose.'

The others were silent.

'I'd love to ride a dragon,' Darrix said. 'What's it like?'

She didn't know how to tell him about tearing through clouds and feeling the wind rip against her face, seeing the ground fall away like it never mattered. Hearing the steady, strong wing beats of a beast too powerful to let you fall.

'… Unforgettable,' she finally said.

***

A little while later they came upon two armed guards, though they both looked quite young, and a robed wizard they knew from the college – one of the older students of

 By Dr Joseph Ireland "Dr Joe"

Sagemaster De'Feur. They appeared to be standing guard over a small tomb marker and a collection of flowers.

'Greetings, Piex. Greetings, all,' the wizard said in a cheery voice.

Piex stuttered his broom to a stop before looking to see who had greeted him. 'Oh. Marchan. Salutations. I … actually, what are you doing out here?'

Marchan smiled. He was about seventeen years old, a year into becoming a full adult. 'Lucid as always, I see, Piex. Actually, the steward has asked me to supplement his royal guard here. We're charged with protecting this **valuable** shrine to Theiss, goddess of roads.'

'That's the shrine?' Kialessa asked in surprise. It was a little more than a stake pressed into the ground with some flowers around it.

'It is indeed!' Marchan said with false flair and pride, making the whole situation seem even funnier with his silliness.

'But why?' Allastassia asked in frustration. 'Anyone would agree it's ridiculous to put two armed guards and a **wizard** and over a tiny marker like this!'

'No,' Darrix said firmly, and the others stopped laughing. 'It is not. The High King wants to remove all gods but the Pantheon, and his servants are after this shrine too. King Dunnkan feels greatly for the mother who lost her son here. This is not a light thing. Not at all.'

Marchan stopped joking too, but still smiled. 'Right

you are, young Darrix. The High King has threatened all such shrines and King Dunnkan is wise to protect those he values. We live in perilous times.'

'More perilous than we know sometimes,' Darrix said with a frown.

'Well, this still seems a little over the top,' the enchantress said. 'You don't think two armed guards and a wizard's apprentice – no offence.'

'None taken,' Marchan smiled.

'Is not excessive? A single guard at best,' she said, correcting the King's policy for him.

Kialessa looked at the three of them. The guards had sat down and were playing cards and didn't seem interested in any of them at all.

'Well,' Marchan said, seeming to want to lighten the mood again. 'Piex, you really freaked us out the other day with your new golden shackles spell. That's impressive magic.' He turned to them, grinning. 'Takes all us other apprentices our full measure of adulthood to even master the basics. Piex here exceeds us all and he's only ten years old! We fear he'll be blowing us away with the *fiery conflagration* before he's even a senior student.'

'Is that why so few of the students want to challenge us anymore?' Piex asked innocently. It was a good point. Few of the senior students looked forward to challenging them nowadays, and then only with superior numbers. They all waited for the answer.

Marchan paused before answering, but then smiled once more. 'That and the fact that we're all sick of having our bones broken by your half troll! Where's he gone? Oh, there he is – never far away. What's his name again?'

'Posk,' Darrix said quickly. Posk had been chasing rabbits with his drake again, who never seemed to pause for very long. The animal seemed to be able to understand about as much conversation as Posk did. Posk enjoyed everyone's company and knew when people were kind enough to be his friend. Besides, he'd been in practice battles with them every Lumday for half a year, which was what Marchan was referring to.

'Posk? Is that his real name?'

'I think it's more of a title,' Darrix said.

'I thought it was his name,' Allastassia replied.

'No, it's just the name he answers to,' Kialessa explained. She was considered the local expert on the strange, green nine-year-old.

'What's his real name?' Marchan asked.

She shrugged, and no one else seemed to know. What did it matter, if Posk was all he answered to?

'Oh well,' Marchan said, brushing it aside. 'Lucky his parents didn't know about horses or they might have called him "Horse"!'

They laughed, and Posk did too, though Kialessa was sure he had no idea why.

Then Marchan's face grew serious. 'Hello, what's

this?'

He motioned to the guards, who jumped up to attention.

From down the path a trio of individuals scurried in a businesslike fashion. With a stab of concern, Kialessa saw it was the second messenger. She approached with crisp fervour and spoke with short, impatient sentences. 'Wizard, stand aside. I am on the missive of the High King to remove this abominable shrine at once.'

When Marchan spoke, it was without a trace of the jocular friendliness of only moments ago. 'I'm sorry, your grace. But I cannot allow you or any of your servants to touch this shrine to the goddess Theiss in any way. King Dunnkan has given me the strictest instructions –'

'King Dunnkan is operating outside the jurisdiction of his own authority. I speak for the High King,' she said curtly. 'Now stand aside while we remove this disgrace or suffer the consequences.'

'I am sorry,' Marchan repeated, without a trace of fear. 'I cannot stand aside without King Dunnkan's express command. My word demands it.' His face was stern, but his voice polite.

The woman gasped in exasperation and surprise. 'You will move, or I will move you.'

Kialessa was worried. She saw Piex's hand slipping into his pockets where his magic spell components lay, and even Allastassia's hand begun to glow as she

                By Dr Joseph Ireland "Dr Joe"

gathered arcane energy, whether she was aware of it or not. Things could turn nasty, very quickly.

'I'm sorry you feel that way,' Marchan replied, then cast a spell. A single bright ball of light exploded upwards.

The messenger cringed as though he was casting at her, but regained her composure quickly. She pulled a rod from her robes. 'Since that is the way you like it, I'll be forced to use this. But don't worry, the paralysis should wear off within a few hours.'

From behind her, Kialessa heard a familiar crack, *Whoosh!*

'STOP!' King Dunnkan roared.

He was standing holding the arm of the Sagemaster, the two of them having only just teleported in. There was no greater authority or power in the entire kingdom.

'King Dunnkan!' The messenger fawned apologetically, 'I'm surprised. I mean, I'm very glad it's you. This misguided wizard here thinks –'

'This wizard is doing exactly what I've instructed him to do,' the king said.

The messenger was almost speechless. 'But he's standing in the way of the High King's order. You must make him to step aside.'

'No.'

'But …' she stammered, 'King Dunnkan, please. This shrine is considered illegal in all other kingdoms of the

Great Kingdom. You must take it down.'

'Or what?'

She grew angry. 'Or you will bring down the wrath of the High King on your whole kingdom! It is *rebellion*, I tell you. You cannot insist that *your* people believe differently to the *whole* great Kingdom.'

'Actually, I believe I can do just that. There is no harm in allowing my people to choose who they worship, so long as it doesn't interfere with other people's freedom. Yet it seems the High King has decided he can do that very thing – he has decreed that we all have to worship **his** gods. I tell you; it is immoral. It is wrong and I and my people will have *no part* in it.'

The messenger was silent, then smiled. 'We thought you might feel that way.' She clicked her fingers at her scholars and walked swiftly away.

They were all silent till King Dunnkan adjusted his robe. 'I'm sorry you young ones had to see that.' He said to them, looking at Kialessa and Allastassia when he did.

'We knew it was coming,' Darrix said, perhaps only really speaking for himself.

'What happens now?' Piex asked.

The Sagemaster smiled at him but said nothing.

Eventually, King Dunnkan spoke again, 'I suppose I get one of you to give me a ride back into town.'

Allastassia offered him her magical Posk in an instant, and King Dunnkan continued to explain as he mounted

     By Dr Joseph Ireland "Dr Joe"

it. 'We really only planned the journey out. Yet as for you young ones … you might like to ask your parents to make sure they have any symbols or shrines to any gods not "approved" well hidden. I think we can expect a visit from the High King's men very soon.'

Kialessa waited till he was out of hearing before asking Darrix, 'What will that mean?'

'Trouble,' he replied. 'Big trouble.'

The army of the High King

Tribulations are to conviction what air is to fire: It extinguishes the weak ones and fans the true.
– High priest of Serros, 4CY.

It all happened exactly one week later.

It had been a busy day at the market. Kialessa was helping carry thirteen bread loaves, a full baker's dozen, with Allastassia's servants when she first heard a commotion.

It was a messenger, and he headed right up to the town square to stand on the podium in the early evening light. 'By order of the steward Lord Grudon, harken well!' he shouted with impressive volume. 'Docked this morn a military force consisting of three hundred warriors from the High kingdom!'

People gasped.

'Why are they here!' the swineherds wife shouted.

'Isn't it obvious!' A man roared over the gathering voices. 'They're here to put down all shrines and symbols not of the approved Pantheon once and for all.'

'But an entire legion!' a woman shouted. 'Three hundred men from the High King's Royal guard. That's equal to King Dunnkan's standing army, only more elite!'

'It could mean violence,' someone shouted in a worried voice.

'It could mean war,' the first man agreed.

'They must have been waiting just outside the boarders of Lenmer'el,' Allastassia whispered to her.

'What are we to do!' A man shouted.

'King Dunnkan has called for calm!' The herald bellowed. 'This is **not** war, this is **not** the time to panic! He had hoped, we had all hoped, that the High King would see reason before it comes to this. But apparently not. Now our king bids you, return to your homes immediately. Destroy or hide any items you have that you fear may offend the army of the High King. Do not impede them in any way, but keep clear and honest records of any distress or damage they do to you or your family…'

He was saying more, but his words were drowned out in the panic that rapidly overtook the crowd. Some began snatching at food, refusing to pay. The town guard moved in to arrest them.

Kialessa and Allastassia were quickly pushed to the edge of the chaos.

'And the first thing to go,' Allastassia said sadly, 'will be the roadside shrine to the goddess of roads.'

From deep amidst the fear and confusion, Kialessa felt rather than heard a chilling laugh. It was soft, almost inaudible. Like a whisper, or a wisp of dank, oppressive air.

She fell to the ground as someone pushed past her. Allastassia was nowhere to be seen. Kialessa looked around, but couldn't seem to make sense of what was happening. She continued to look around her as she walked along in numb disbelief, making her way slowly through the city. To her surprise, she found the main street blocked by several overturned carts. Men with pitchforks and clubs were working among it trying to build a blockade. It looked like they were digging in for a fight. Perhaps that was the right thing to do? Or perhaps it would only make things worse? But it seemed to be what everyone else was doing, and before she knew it, she found she had a torn plank in her hand, and was bringing it to the men to use.

        By Dr Joseph Ireland "Dr Joe"

Horns sounded, and the warriors at the barricade grabbed up their pitchforks.

'Drop your weapons!' a voice shouted. It was Honoured Lord Bon Sure'e, the captain of the king's guard. He rode up with a dozen other elite soldiers on his battle scarred posk. 'Fools, disband at once! Do you wish to bring this doom on us all!'

'I'd rather die than live under this law!' a man shouted back.

'You fear the High King's foolish decree! Coward!' Another man shouted at the captain.

At that, Bon Sure'e drew steel. The crowed fell silent, holding their breath. Someone pushed the man forward who'd called the most famous warrior in the kingdom of Lenmer'el a coward. He was an old man, yet he faced the captain without fear.

Bon Sure'e rode up, and eyed him closely, his drawn sword within arm's reach. Nobody moved.

'None live that have called me that, farmhand,' the captain said in insult. 'I see it is your wish to die today. Well let me tell you, if you continue to build this barricade in an attempt to oppose the High King's men that is exactly what will happen to you. And not only you. Perhaps the legion will decide this whole street, maybe this whole city, is in league with you. What if they decide to burn it all to the ground because of the pride of a single man? I am warning you, old man. Stand aside, and all those with you, least you bring down war on your families!'

Most people dropped their tools, but the old man stood resolute. For a moment the air was still until the old man broke the silence, 'Never,' he told the captain.

'Arrest this man,' Bon Sure'e ordered, and in an instant he was bound by the soldiers. Then the captain ran his war posk right at the barricade, and it began ripping it to shreds with its powerful claws and sharp teeth.

Within moments there were very few people on that street.

Kialessa moved on, making her way towards the castle. There, all was chaos as well. Cutlery was being burnt, images scoured off and scripture incinerated. From outside the high castle windows Kialessa watched several caravans heading towards the outlying hamlets. People were even fleeing. They were accompanied by small processions of downcast people taking only what they could carry to the relative safety of the deep woods. There would be little but their determination and swords to protect them in there, but they must have felt safer within, than in the path of an army.

Then Kialessa seemed to come to herself, the high up view helping her realise she needed to be somewhere else. She ran then, down towards the college.

But she soon found the students were walking the other way. College had been dismissed, and the head

     By Dr Joseph Ireland "Dr Joe"

mistress was too busy to notice as she scurried about in a great fuss making sure every piece of linen and parchment was free of the stain of any but the "correct" beliefs. Even Thyme, a valuable herb that was associated with the goddess of autumn, faced the fire. Only one college tutor had the courage to keep a small box of it, carefully labelled *for educational purposes only.* Kialessa took the opportunity to slip away from the worried throng and head out to the surrounding village.

Three hundred soldiers of the High Kingdom. Everyone was worried.

As she rushed down through the town Kialessa soon discovered the busiest building within the walls. In every disaster, it seemed, someone would find a way to make a profit. And he who seemed to be profiting most from the rebellion of King Dunnkan was Darrix's father.

His workshop was in overdrive. Kialessa watched in shock as they melted down authentic coins of the High Kingdom and poured the scorching metal into the new moulds of the Pantheon. Hundreds of people were there. One man grabbed at the new medallions even before they'd had time to cool, crying out as the burning metal scalded his hands. There were nobles and peasants; everyone wanted to be found with a medallion in their homes or on their person when the army arrived.

This is madness. Kialessa thought to herself, and slipped around the back till she could see Darrix through one of the windows. He had to distract the men he was with before he found the chance to slip away to talk to her.

'What is happening?' she said, and was surprised to hear the fear in her own voice.

Darrix, however, seemed completely calm. 'This is madness,' he muttered. 'As soon as father hears about the army he runs out into the street and hires six new workers. He's melting everything down to make those stupid medallions. He's even melted down every sword at the workshop and people are still purchasing them like crazy. He'll be a rich man again by the time the day is out.'

'I saw them melting down coins, is that legal?'

'No, but I think given the circumstances, the High King will forgive the act. At least, that's what my father expects.'

'How can they expect to buy their relationship with the gods?'

'They're not. Not really. No one is going to abandon their old beliefs, just become very public about the Pantheon. They're not buying a relationship with a god; they're buying peace with an army.'

'Do you think King Dunnkan will stand up to the High King's men?'

'Nobody expects it. King Dunnkan is strong and his army well trained, but no one in all the High Kingdom is individually powerful enough to challenge the High King. It would mean their death and the destruction of

     By Dr Joseph Ireland "Dr Joe"

hundreds in any one realm. Nobody expects King Dunnkan to stand up to the High King with anything more than angry words.'

'He is a good man.'

'That's why I hope he doesn't pick a fight. He's too good a man to lose as king.'

They were silent while shouts of angry and hurried customers could be heard from the other rooms.

'People are afraid,' Kialessa thought out loud to herself.

'They have good reason to be.'

Kialessa looked out at the dusty workshop, filled with frantic and frightened people. The sound of their fears was barely drowned out the by thunder of the furnace and the ringing of metal as strong arms brought hammers down on scalding steel, arms that could well be wielding swords by the next dawn.

'Then ... do you think some of King Dunnkan's people will put up a fight?'

8 At the window

Darrix turned to face her, his expression grim. 'Some will, undoubtedly. That's one of the hard things about standing up for what you believe in; should you be gentle and convincing, or violent and demanding? Both have their natural results. Sometimes people put up a fight and sometimes it's not about winning a war but simply hurting others. I hope they don't fight the High King's men. In matters of faith, it's impossible to believe something more powerful doesn't know exactly what's going on. Turning to violence would usually, I think, simply get in the way of achieving something good.'

'Will you fight?'

'Never,' Darrix replied. 'Unless it is necessary in self-

 By Dr Joseph Ireland "Dr Joe"

defence, and even then maybe not. Adding violence to violence makes no sense. Even farmers know you don't fight fire with fire, you fight fire by burning away the fuel before the fire even gets there. Take away the fuel, offer a peaceful solution, and the fight may be over before it has even begun.'

She thought he sounded very sage, and hoped they'd find a peaceful solution to this madness soon.

'You'd better go see Posk is all right,' he said. 'They won't understand him. And maybe you'd better go wait out in the forest too, for a few days, just to make sure …'

'No, I need to see this through.'

'As you wish.'

'I guess you'd better get back to work, then.'

'Where will you go, Kia?'

She didn't know until he'd asked. 'I need to check on King Dunnkan, for when the High King's men arrive.'

She touched his hand and he held hers in sympathy. Then they both ran off to do what they felt had to be done.

***

The High King's men were there within hours. Three hundred pennants of gold and purple fluttering in the breeze might have been an exciting sight any other day, but instead the people watched them with great apprehension. The castle guards allowed the royal army right into the castle without a word of complaint.

That was when Kialessa saw the third messenger. He was unlike the others; small, with handsome eyes and soft brown hair. He rode in a gilded carriage with several other officials, including a powerful looking wizard and several high-ranking clerics of the old Pantheon. She only glimpsed him as they rode up the street to the castle keep, lined with King Dunnkan's men, all of whom were fully armed.

The High King's men stood at attention, the radiant gleam of their polished helms and armour making them appear surrounded by a glittering barrier of solid will. They were glorious and terrifying, all at once.

A herald stood out from the High King's men. 'Noble house of King Dunnkan! The messenger of his High and Royal Lordship, Noblest of Kings, the High King, seeks permission to discuss matters regarding the High Kingdom at the congeniality of King Dunnkan's court!'

It was an official greeting. They could have just walked in but were following protocol by asking permission they probably didn't need.

A call responded from the keep. It was the steward. 'His Lordship and Keeper of the People, King Dunnkan, graciously and kindly greets all messengers of his goodness, the High King, and bids them, as valued friends and family, to share the bounty of his table this day.'

        By Dr Joseph Ireland "Dr Joe"

It was so polite it made everything seem unreal. But people still had good reason to be afraid; if the army decided they didn't like what they found …

The gates opened and an entourage of about twenty people, including some heavily armoured royal guards, entered the keep. The rest of the High King's royal army waited perfectly in line, as though ready to respond to orders in an instant.

Kialessa knew she had little time, so she raced along ahead of the High King's messenger through all the short cuts, across a windowsill and up a stand of ivy. She reached the doors of the throne room quickly.

'Let me in,' she begged. She was officially allowed to see the king whenever she wanted. One of the soldiers looked like he disagreed, but another one simply nodded and let her in.

She raced in and found King Dunnkan suited in his royal outfit, golden sword at his waist, conferring with his counsellors.

'King Dunnkan!' Kialessa shouted and flung herself into his arms.

'Of all the times, child!' said the steward, exasperated.

'It's all right, Kialessa. We've done all we can do and must leave the rest up to the Eternal himself. I must keep the High King's law.'

'I know.' She hid a sob that rose unbidden within her.

'Eminence!' a voice from the entry called. 'The

messenger approaches.'

'Already?' Kialessa and the king said at the same time.

'Quickly, hide yourself!' The king instructed.

She looked around for a place to hide. Then the wizard, who was also there, looked up at the tapestry. He winked. Did he know she'd been there a dozen times before? Could she keep a secret from him at all?

She climbed up just one instant before the first of the High King's honour guard marched into the throne room.

Holding her breath, she peered out from behind the tapestry. Both groups were putting on a show of power and numbers. King Dunnkan, his royal family, six or seven of the most powerful nobles and all the elite warriors were there. They were greeted by an equally powerful and noble line up of soldiers and officials from the High Kingdom. Two high priests, a wizard, and Tomin the paladin were among them.

'King Dunnkan –' the herald began.

'Dispense with the pleasantries!' King Dunnkan ordered, and the herald fell silent. The mood in the room tensed. 'You have come to enforce the edict of the High King to oppress my people's religious expression with unnecessary and unrighteous law. Get to the point and tell me what you are going to do.'

The handsome, small man with brown eyes and chestnut hair stood forward. 'I am the High King's messenger, and it was at my council that the High King has enacted this righteous law for the benefit of the whole Great Kingdom, so it is I that he sends to enforce this law here. It is a most unfortunate thing that you have done, King Dunnkan. Unfortunate and unnecessary. The High King's edict was made abundantly clear to you, and you have failed to comply on every account. Your rebellion is costing him greatly, not to mention you encourage dissidence among the other kingdoms. It is a wonder to me why the High King does not order you to renounce your kingship immediately.'

King Dunnkan's captain stepped forward and moved his hand to grasp the hilt of his sword. It was a motion he allowed everyone to see. 'None may threaten my king in his own throne room.'

'Nevertheless,' the messenger continued with greater caution, 'for reasons of his own kindness, his High Goodness has decided to allow you to keep your kingdom and to continue to rule your people as you see fit. He has, however, authorised me to stay as long as is necessary, and to do whatever is required to ensure the old Pantheon is honoured as appropriate among **all** the people of the High Kingdom. It is necessary, for their peace.'

King Dunnkan scowled. 'You will burn their families' heirlooms? You will dishonour the memories of their ancestors? You will deny grieving mothers the graves of their sons? You will take from them the right to choose their beliefs? You call that having peace?'

'I will do whatever is necessary to ensure the edict of the High King is fulfilled *to the letter*,' the messenger replied with a strict tone, but his voice was almost kind. He seemed to only want to do his job properly and well.

The throne room was silent for a while. When King Dunnkan spoke, the anxiety and sorrow was evident in his own voice. 'I will not impede you in any way, but if you hurt **any** of the people, if you so much as cut the hair off an old widow, you **will** feel the wrath of my indignation.'

'I have given the High King my word that not one of your people will be harmed in any way – that is, any that do not draw weapons to stop us. But we must insist we begin with your own chapel, adorning it with the appropriate icons of worship. And I believe you keep a shrine to some "Eternal" for the servants? We will begin to dismantle it immediately.'

'You will forgive me,' King Dunnkan replied, 'if I do not join you for the feast in the High King's honour tonight? My appetite has quite left me.'

'As you wish, for you are king.' The messenger replied in a voice both smooth and kind, but his words made Kialessa wonder if he really was hiding something more … cruel.

Kialessa heard no more; she was already running out of the window and climbing down the walls. She didn't care if the guards saw her, she just ran. She ran right past

 By Dr Joseph Ireland "Dr Joe"

the armed and wary guards of King Dunnkan, right past the nearly three hundred alert and silent soldiers of the High King. She ran right to the store where Darrix's father was still making a great profit.

She burst in screaming, 'Darrix, they're going to destroy the shrine to the Eternal!'

It was something that, in hindsight, she probably shouldn't have done.

He dropped his hammer and ran out.

'Stop right where you are, son!' his father roared.

Darrix did not reply. He ran up to a nearby well and yanked off the chain, sending the bucket down into the depths. He didn't stop, and in moments he was far ahead of Kialessa and running hard. His father came out then, and shouted angrily at him. But there were a lot of customers. And they all had money to buy things.

She did not know what Darrix was doing or why he'd grabbed the chain, but she soon found out. She caught up to him at the shrine of the Eternal. It was a beautiful and simple shine where she and Darrix would go to worship once a week and read out the deeds done in the Eternal's name, and discuss and disagree about how to apply those words in their own lives. Kialessa gasped at the bright white flames that wreathed the circle of the Eternal and the boy who had **chained** himself to it.

'Darrix …' she said.

'Darrix, what are you doing?' The cleric of the shrine

rushed in at the same moment, also looking worried.

'Priestess!' Darrix said. 'They're coming to break down the shrine of the Eternal. They will hurt you. You must flee!'

'I will not.'

'But you can't stop them!' Kialessa said. She was sure she could hear the soldiers already and still didn't know what Darrix was trying to do.

'I won't try. I've always wanted to be a gardener,' the Priestess said calmly and smiled.

'You're a terrible gardener,' Darrix said.

'I know. But I will not be a priest to any other god. But you, Darrix, what are you doing?'

'Chaining myself to the circle. You might not resist them, but I will. Oh, I won't fight them, but I won't let them take the circle of the Eternal away.'

She nodded 'Darrix, are you sure you are called to resist this evil?'

'I feel like I should, priestess. This feels... I should.'

'Do you see the fire of the eternal about you?'

'I do,' Kialessa replied.

And with that, Darrix clicked a lock into place and gave the key to the old priestess.

'As you wish,' the old dwarf smiled, and then they could hear them. The armoured soldiers were approaching.

The first to enter, without even bowing, barely

paused. 'By the High King's edict, all religions not of the old Pantheon are to put down and their religious artefacts destroyed. Stand aside, old woman.'

'I will not resist the edict of the High King.'

'Then remove your sacrilegious robes.'

The priestess sighed, but did not move.

So the soldiers were brutal. They tore the cloak off her without a word of apology, knocking her to the ground, and burnt it immediately. Then they dragged her out and made her show them where all the other religious items were kept and they burnt them too. One by one, they took the pews from the building; the nice ones they sold for the High King's coffers and the older ones they cut up for firewood. Then they turned their attention to the circle.

'You boy, get away from there!' The soldier said.

'No,' Darrix replied.

'Unlock yourself or I'll break your arms doing it myself.'

'No you won't!' Kialessa replied. 'You aren't allowed to harm any of King Dunnkan's people. I heard the messenger say so myself.'

'How would you have heard … never mind. Soldiers, cut this boy's chain immediately and drag him away.'

'No!' Darrix shouted, preparing himself to kick away at the guards.

But he could not last long at this.

Then Kialessa had an idea. She reached into one of the

many little hidden pockets in her leather armour. There was a small keepsake she'd acquired once, not long ago, after meeting a moon dragon and saving it from a magical chain by cutting it with another magical chain – a chain imbued with goodness. She tossed the three tiny silver links onto the old well chain that held Darrix to the circle, and it dissolved into the larger chain like butter on a hot stove. Suddenly all the rust and dirt melted off the old well chain and it now stood bright and fervent as the day it was forged.

One of the High King's guards swung an axe and attempted to sever it. His swing left a great notch in the axe and not a scratch on the chain.

'It's not letting me out till I tell it to,' Darrix explained, his smile beaming at all the success he was having.

The guard swung again and again, and each time managed to only cut great chips out of his weapon till at last it was blunt.

'Where's the key?' The soldier shouted.

'It's gone. I don't have it and I don't know where it is,' Darrix replied, which was all quite true.

Another solider reached out to grab Kialessa but she slipped away. He ran to grab her again but she sprinted along the ceiling skirting board as three more of them leapt at her only to find their hands empty. Finally, she jumped right on the side of the great circle and held on, her eyes glowing an angry red as she hissed at the soldiers with her forked tongue and they all jumped back.

'Ahh … get the messenger!' The soldier in charge ordered.

He was there in moments. 'What seems to be the problem?'

The guard pointed, and then the messenger entered only a few paces to look at the now vacant shrine, vacant all except for a boy chained to a wooden pillar and a tae'anaryn girl so agile no one had managed to catch her yet.

The messenger looked around and smiled calmly. 'Take everything else down, and leave the boy there if he insists.'

That's exactly what they did.

The vigil

Recognising a true cause, driven by solid commitment,
is easy to judge – it is no effort at all.
– Nemon, 3rd sage of Lumos

Kialessa eventually found herself cornered by one of the guards, stopping her at sword point. He took her to see the head mistress, who was busy trying to keep the remaining, terrified, students busy and clean. She kept Kialessa busy for several hours, but when more soldiers turned up and began asking questions Kialessa managed to slip away. When she did, it was a crushing blow to her heart to see what they'd done to the shrine where she worshipped. They'd taken all the tiles off the roof and had begun bashing all the walls down. Some men were removing the rubble right up to the cobbled stones that were once the shrine's floor. A small crowd had gathered, both to mourn the shrine, and to see the young boy still chained up to a pillar, now burning gold with holy flames it seemed no one except Kialessa could see.

Darrix was standing now, bold and dignified. He was not going to move while the circle still stood.

'Darrix, I –' she started to say.

'DARRIX!' It was his father. He stormed past Kialessa and almost knocked her over, bringing with him six armed workers from his forge.

'What is this nonsense? You workers,' he said to the High King's guard who were still dismantling the shrine, 'cease your labours and let me in to talk some sense to my boy!'

They shrugged and the one in charge told them to down tools for the time being. They walked out, someone muttering something about hoping for a cup of hot cocoa.

Darrix said nothing.

His father was livid. 'Darrix,' he said, getting close, 'I want you out of those chains this instant.'

'No.'

'You'll unlock those chains this moment or so help me!'

'Sorry, Father. I can't leave until the High King changes his mind.'

Darrix's father was so furious now he put his finger right up to his son's face. 'You'll cut yourself out now or so help me boy … you stand to lose your inheritance.'

'I don't **need** my inheritance!' Darrix shouted back, then regained his composure. 'I don't need your gold, Father. I need my faith. I am sorry I cannot be the son you want me to be and you're just going to have to live with that. I am going to stay in these chains until the High King realises he's –'

Then the old man slapped him.

'Get out of those chains or you can find your own home to live in.'

The crowd was silent. It was the worst threat a father could offer a child, and to lose a home …

'I'm sorry, Father.' Darrix looked down and sighed. Then he looked his father again in the eye.

With distain and disgust, Darrix's father threw his hands in the air. 'Do what you will,' he said to the High King's men.

Kialessa gasped and ran to Darrix's side. 'You can't leave him like that!' she said to his father.

'Why not? What is he to me?'

Darrix simmered in unspoken anger for many hours, till the whole crowd had left, and he and Kialessa were alone in the empty field that was once a shrine to the Eternal.

***

          By Dr Joseph Ireland "Dr Joe"

Piex came by soon after, while they waited in silence for a king to come to his senses. They were otherwise alone, and it was beginning to get dark, so they were glad to see he'd brought blankets.

'Thank you, Piex,' Kialessa said.

Darrix nodded.

'Have you taken an oath of silence?' Piex asked.

'No,' Darrix said, 'but it's … uncomfortable. We're fasting, however. How are things in the villages?'

Piex paused before answering. 'There's been no blood shed, at least not to my knowledge … yet. But the High King's men are tearing the place apart looking for statues, figurines or even letters signed in the name of any god but the seven. They took old Father Brunhall's home and burnt it to the ground after he refused to take away the images of Winter from his home. It was his wife's favourite deity. He says she brought them together. King Dunnkan's men had to hold him down to prevent him from rushing into the flames.'

'That's cruel,' Kialessa said.

Piex didn't smile. 'They cut down all the groves to Myala and had to drive the people out at sword point. I think there would definitely be blood spilt if it wasn't for King Dunnkan's men –'

'Was there fighting?' Kialessa asked.

'No. Not yet. But there's nothing anyone can do. King Dunnkan's men walk around in small groups and when any of the High King's men see them they tend to go a bit more gently. That's all. I'm sorry to live to see this.'

'How is the king?' Darrix asked.

'He's at his throne, where everyone thinks he should be. I think he's fasting too. He … he only had bread and water for dinner. That's food for prisoners.' Piex eyes grew wet with tears. 'Bread and water for our King!'

Kialessa screamed in frustration. 'How can the High King do this? He must know that King Dunnkan and his people will never take to beliefs they didn't choose. If anything, this will make people *hate* the old Pantheon even more!'

No one argued with her.

***

Posk arrived shortly after Piex left and looked quizzically at the boy tied up to the pillar.

'Evening, Posk,' Kialessa said.

He grunted and pointed at the chain.

'Yes, Darrix tied himself up.'

'Greetings, Posk,' Darrix said. He sounded a little tired.

Posk scurried to them, looking around carefully, as though he expected someone to attack him. He had a few scratches on his arm as if he'd been in a scuffle, but there was no point asking him about it.

He reached Darrix and pulled at the chains.

'No, Posk. I'm staying.'

Posk pulled harder, as though he was trying to figure out how to rip them from the pillar.

'No!' Darrix ordered and tried to pull them from Posk's hands. In the process, he jarred the young half troll's fingers. 'Sorry!' he said quickly.

The half troll looked at him, confused, making a querying sound with his voice.

Darrix sighed. 'I'm staying here till the High King changes his mind. I've chained myself to this pillar because I don't believe I can be told who to worship.'

Posk looked into his face. There was no way the disabled boy could understand what Darrix was saying, but he must have understood something by the way he said it. He scurried away.

'He's a good boy,' Darrix muttered.

A moment later, Posk hurried back, carrying a bowl of some soup in his overlarge hands. It smelt ordinary but to the young fasting Darrix, it must have smelled wonderful.

'No, Posk,' he said.

Posk offered him the soup anyway.

Kialessa moved the bowl away from him. 'Sorry, Posk. We're not eating either.'

Posk looked confused again. He might not have understood what was going on, but he must have known that terrible things were happening all over town.

Kialessa knew he would be worried about the fact his friend had chained himself to a pole. But there was no way of knowing what Posk was thinking; he didn't speak.

With a growl, he threw the bowl to the floor and it shattered. He looked up at Darrix in anger and frustration, then he raced off in the direction of the forest, the walls echoing with his fast-retreating footsteps.

She felt so sorry for him.

'He's a good boy,' Darrix repeated.

***

For a long time there was silence.

'Aren't we too young for this kind of thing?' Darrix suddenly asked.

It was night now and the blankets weren't keeping them quite as warm as they used to. The gold fire still burnt around the circle but it had dimmed – just a bit. A moment later some of the High King's men came by, probably on their way to report their tyranny to the messenger. They laughed when they saw Darrix.

'Go away!' Kialessa shouted.

But that only made them laugh more.

But their mocking laughter stopped short when one of them saw some others approaching. They left quickly.

It was a small procession of nobles. Allastassia, her parents and some others, probably servants.

     By Dr Joseph Ireland "Dr Joe"

'Oh, Darrix!' Allastassia said, and ran up and threw her arms around him. 'So it's true? What have they done here?' Her bright blue eyes were filled with tears.

'You're a brave young man,' her father said to Darrix. He was Lord Tar Greenhaven, a tall half-oak with dark hazel eyes and a seemingly ageless, penetrating gaze. Her mother, Lady Annadaria, was an enchantress of much fame. Tall and attractive, she was dressed in blue and silver robes that enhanced her seemingly endless beauty. Kialessa has seen them both in the throne room of the king when the third messenger had arrived.

'He tied himself to the circle this morning, as soon as the messenger began to tear the place apart,' Kialessa explained.

Allastassia's mother touched the chain. 'It is enchanted.'

Kialessa nodded.

The parents looked at each other.

'Will you take it off?' she asked Darrix in a very straightforward manner.

'No.'

Allastassia's parents looked at each other again.

'Oh, Darrix, it's the same all over town,' Allastassia cried. 'The High King's men are making a right mess of things. It's awful!'

'Don't worry,' he said. 'Everything will work out for the best.'

'I could really use your faith right now.' She hugged him again. 'What will you do?'

'I'm staying right here till the High King changes his mind.'

Allastassia was visibly upset by this. 'No, please don't Darrix. You'll d– you'll make yourself ill. You shouldn't.'

'Don't!' he said forcefully, but then calmed down. 'I must.'

'Daddy, please give Darrix your ring, the one that keeps you warm,' Allastassia said.

'No,' Darrix and Allastassia's father said at almost the same moment.

Darrix explained. 'I'm fasting. I will take no enchanted protection.'

'I expected as much,' her father said in an understanding voice.

'But Darrix!' Allastassia protested.

'We'll be all right,' Kialessa said.

'Are you fasting too?' Allastassia asked.

She nodded.

'But you can't stay here, Kialessa. You have to come back to our place. *You* can't stay here.'

'Oh, I'm staying with D–'

'Go, Kialessa,' Darrix ordered.

That made her feel frustrated because he thought he could tell her what to do, but mostly that he was trying to stop her from helping him.

'I don't think –'

But he spoke with sudden fervour and authority. 'You can't stay here tonight, Kialessa. It's not right for me to keep you here. This is **my** battle. Go with Allastassia.'

Even if Kialessa could have kept the tears from her eyes, she couldn't keep the sorrow from her voice. 'Darrix, I want to stay and protect the shrine too.'

Darrix shook his head and looked up at the stars where a shine roof once stood. 'Not tonight. I want you to go. Sleep in a bed. Be back tomorrow.'

'Darrix you –'

'It's not like I'm going anywhere.'

Now she wanted to slap him for making light of things. For trying to tell her what to do. But most of all for making her leave him when she was needed.

'Come with us, Kialessa.' Allastassia's mother spoke in a soft, kind voice. 'We will leave some of the servants to watch over him during the night.'

There was little she could do to resist.

'Why?' she asked Darrix.

'Because I'll be happier knowing you're safe.'

Then, though she rarely did, she hugged him too. 'I don't want to go.'

'I know.'

And she allowed herself to be led away.

***

Allastassia's mansion was beautiful, except for the great burn marks in the front lawn where a pile of materials had been heaped and incinerated. Allastassia's mother saw her looking at it sadly.

'I could have stopped them,' she explained, 'but there is no wisdom in bringing down the High King's wrath on our people at this time.'

They took Kialessa past seven or eight rooms into a kitchen, where a cook hurried to fix a simple meal, long past the hours of her usual employ.

Kialessa sat eating her bread quietly. On any other day the fresh wholemeal rolls would have tasted fantastic, and the spicy cheeses exciting. But this was not that day.

'I hear they took down a whole side of the Gwynnore's manor.' Allastassia said, looking like she was sharing news just to make conversation.

Kialessa found it hard to be interested in anyone else's problems right now. 'Is everyone here all right?' Kialessa finally asked.

'Well, they took away chef Hundlono's family crest. He's had that in his family for three generations, but the carvings are all of gnome and woodland deity. We couldn't hide it soon enough and they're using a priest's compass to find all the best hiding places.'

Kialessa didn't want to talk anymore, so she just sat, tasting her bread in miserable sadness.

     By Dr Joseph Ireland "Dr Joe"

Allastassia watched her for a moment, then took her by the hand and led her into the waiting room. It was richly decorated, with expensive leather couches and thick silk curtains. But the main feature was an enormous carved relief of the family crest, depicting dozens of individuals working, resting and playing.

'Mother updates it with her enchantments every year,' Allastassia said.

It was a great work of art, but Kialessa wasn't really interested in art right now. 'I'm surprised the High King's men let you keep it,' Kialessa said bitterly. 'They're burning everything else that people value right now.'

Allastassia looked at her conspiratorially, 'And they should have broken up this too.'

Kialessa was curious. 'Why?'

'Can you keep a secret?'

Kialessa raised an eyebrow. It was the dumbest question in the world!

'All right,' she replied. 'You see the whole family group? Look behind them. What do you see surrounding them?' She pointed to the picture and traced out a circle.

The symbol of the Eternal.

'No way …'

Allastassia put her fingers to Kialessa's lips and nodded. 'Mother has worshiped the Eternal her whole life, even before she moved to this land, as do I.'

'Really? You worship the Eternal too?'

'Yeah. Mother makes us go to King Dunnkan's chapel every Serrosday. It's **so** boring, but I don't really mind, and I get to check out all the latest gossip and the young prince and all. There are some good looking young male nobles, wouldn't you agree?'

Kialessa didn't know what was more surprising, that Allastassia's family had hidden a perfectly obvious symbol to a god right in front of an oppressive army, or that Allastassia was going to church just to check out boys. Perhaps the most surprising thing was that she had chosen the same god as Darrix and herself, and Kialessa hadn't even realised. 'How did you hide it?'

'My sleepy uncle, you remember him? It turns out he's not all that useless after all. As soon as the High King's men walked in and said, "That looks like a circle to the Eternal," he burst out laughing and said, "Next we'll be cutting up our swords because they have straight line, like the goddess of roads!" He made them feel like such fools they walked out again.'

'Really? Is that all?'

'Yep,' Allastassia sighed. 'Some of the best magic isn't even magic at all.' She winked.

Kialessa walked up and touched the circle. A gentle gold fire tingled under her fingertips.

It *was* a circle to the Eternal.

'That's what worries me,' Allastassia said, 'with Darrix. He must know. You can't destroy all the symbols to the gods when any can be drawn in the sand or summoned with a whispered prayer. Why does he need to tie himself to that stupid pillar?'

Kialessa's face flashed hot with anger, but she chose not to show her hostess. She was upset that Allastassia didn't *really* understand what Darrix was trying to do. Then again, perhaps neither did she.

'I think with Darrix,' she replied, looking to the circle for the wisdom to answer her friend well, 'it's more of a public thing. He can't hold his beliefs private. He needs everyone to know. He needs to share what he's found in his faith. It's not something that can pass into the night. Darrix isn't that kind of person.'

Allastassia was silent for a moment. 'I suppose I admire that,' she said, looking away towards the castle.

'He'll stand up for what he believes in, and defend what he feels is worth protecting. But he's not going to force those beliefs on others. Unlike the High King.'

They didn't say much else, and shortly after, retired to bed. Kialessa was given a duck down mattress but she would have given it up for a midnight vigil with her devout friend. She found it hard to get to sleep in a night filled with injustice, but when she did, she slept like a brick.

Vigil
day two

It matters not if you try and fail and try and fail again.
What matters is if you try and fail and fail to try again:
Then quit. No sense being a darn fool about it.
– Humdug, dwarf scholar.

Kialessa woke up before anyone else, and helping herself to some water, left for Darrix's vigil. His mother was there; she'd brought him some kind of cloak. She was tall, with a strong jaw and beautiful face, but it was a face pale with worry.

'**You** will talk some sense into him, won't you dear?'

she pleaded to Kialessa. 'He'll catch his death of cold like this.'

But Kialessa thought Darrix was more sensible then all the king's men, standing up for a good cause. He was praying towards the rising sun. She patted him on the shoulder and he smiled at her while she sat on the ground next to him to help him wait.

They waited a long time, saying nothing, and the sun was high when Piex returned.

'Nothing. Nowhere,' he said with a sorry voice. 'I've checked all the records. I never liked law; I can't get it a page at a time like the sciences of wizardry. But I've been through all the records they let me see and then all the ones they let me see once the sagemaster told them to let me read *everything*. I don't think there's a book in the castle on law that I haven't … hey, did you know that it's actually illegal to own a pig and a dog on the same farm if it grows parsley? I pointed it out to the judge and they're very embarrassed!'

'That's great, Piex,' Darrix said.

Piex did not look pleased. 'I really tried. I looked everywhere to find a flaw in the High King's act. But I can't find any legal reason for him not to do exactly what he's just done.'

Darrix nodded, as if he finally understood where Piex was going with this long, winding conversation. 'I didn't think so,' he said.

'It was good of you to try,' Kialessa agreed. It seemed everyone was helping out in their own way.

'And if he orders you off that pole … it's law Darrix,' Piex said sadly.

'I feared so.'

Kialessa shook her head. 'But there must be *something* we can do. The High King's law can't have been written to let him do *anything*. That's troll law,' Kialessa complained, quoting what they'd been taught at college. 'There should be a law against telling people what they must worship.'

'I suppose there is,' Piex said, 'if you somehow count it against the first laws of the constitution.'

'What do you mean?' Kialessa asked.

'Well, the first laws of the constitution were drafted when the first High King came to power three hundred years ago, and they wrote that one of the first four great rights of all citizens of the High Kingdom is to worship whomever they choose, so long as it doesn't impose on the rights and privileges of others. The new High King must have redefined it to mean just the Pantheon –'

'But he can't do that!' Darrix was excited. 'He'd need a public vote to change the first laws. Look at the precedents. The gods that have been called on number in the hundreds, not just the gods of the Pantheon!'

'Oh, yes, well I suppose …' Piex mused.

'Don't you see? You've got him! You've found the

High King's act of removing all but the Pantheon to be illegal!'

'What?' Piex and Kialessa asked at the same time.

'It's a fundamental right! Tell the king's judges, see what they say! The High King's act goes against the fundamental rights of the High King's people, and he's changed the law without resorting to legal processes!'

'But it can't be that simple. The judges have been figuring this out as much as any –' Kialessa said.

'Actually, I think it can.' Piex said, infected by Darrix's excitement. 'With all the bi-laws and cases built on cases it's no wonder no one's actually looked at the foundation of the law in a while. The simple things often evade in the complex business of law. And there hasn't been a challenge based on the interpretation of the constitution itself in a hundred years, it'd be a landmark case with jury and high judges …'

Piex said no more, but scurried off faster than she knew he could run.

'This is good. This is the shadow of a chance …' Darrix muttered, and adjusted his shoulders.

***

It was mid-afternoon and everyone seemed to have given up on the idea of college for the time being. Kialessa was content keeping Darrix company instead, and there were plenty of visitors and well wishes. And then Tomin came to visit.

Kialessa knew he was coming several moments before he arrived. It may have been the small crowd that accompanied him or the clink of his unique and powerful armour. Then again, perhaps it was simply the aura of authority and might that he wielded; even the dust in the air around him seemed to fall in line.

He rode up on his great grey Posk, looking around at the desolated shrine. His face was difficult to read – a blend of compassion and self-righteousness. He dismissed the people with a wave, and the men at arms that accompanied him everywhere began shooing people away with great haste.

Darrix said nothing. When it was just the three of them, Tomin leaned forward on his saddle. He cast a quick, derisive glance in Kialessa's direction, then spoke to Darrix, 'We'll, young man, seems you've got yourself a bit of a situation here.'

'Honoured. It is good to see you,' Darrix replied, and Kialessa wondered why he was being so polite.

'Tell me,' Tomin said, 'why are you here with this tae'anaryn?'

It made Kialessa's blood boil. Darrix was here to protect his faith. Why would Tomin assume it had something to do with her?

Darrix burst out laughing. 'I tie myself to a pole in

protest of unjust laws and you wonder about the only person willing to stay with me? Search her yourself if you have questions. She can answer for herself.'

Tomin lost his smile. He drew his sword, and they both jumped. It was the Avenger, radiating power and law. It had severed the heads of dragons and dispelled the darkness of vampires. It was known to discern the heart and lies of people and would speak to Tomin from time to time. It was without doubt the most powerful and divine tool in the entire kingdom of Lenmer'el at this time, excepting the rod King Dunnkan held.

Tomin threw one leg over the saddle and jumped down, his Posk bending a knee obediently as though it knew what he was planning before he'd done it. It was an amazing beast, seeming itself sanctified in some way. Its eyes were ever watchful; fearless, and dangerous.

Kialessa cringed, folding her legs up in case she had to run. She couldn't believe he'd **actually** hurt her, not unless he had a reason to.

He stabbed his sword into the stones at his feet and it stood there effortlessly. Then Tomin prayed, 'Serros, brighten the truth of this young tae'anaryn's heart!'

Tomin drew his head back. On his face was an expression of surprise and then perhaps disappointment. With a huff, he pulled Avenger from the ground and turned to Darrix, his mighty posk unmoving behind him.

'And?' Darrix asked.

He glared at Darrix before answering the impertinent question, after all, Tomin was a knight. 'Serros has shown me that she is not the cause of your obstinacy. I will witness that to any who ask further.'

'Is that what people have been asking?'

For a moment Tomin glared, then laughed. He placed Avenger point down in the ground and half leant on the hilt of the sword. 'That, and many more things,' he said with a friendly stare, then began to look around at the desecrated shine in disappointment. 'It did not need to come to this.'

'You mean,' Darrix said, 'the complete and total disregard for my, for anyone's, personal beliefs?'

Tomin did not argue but stared at Darrix once more.

Looking in Tomin's eyes, Kialessa realised something. 'You don't agree with the High King, do you?'

Tomin looked angry, but contained it well. She knew if anyone else had told him that, he would not have been so offended. 'My personal beliefs aside, I am sworn to serve a king. And serve him I will, till my last breath! It is not often I am called to be the easy way, to set an example of piety before an army is called for. But that was the way it was this time and I could not help that. I warned you, didn't I, boy? I warned you that changes are coming and that unity is called for.'

Darrix thought before answering, 'Unity? Or oppression?'

Tomin looked genuinely angry but seemed to think better of it before shouting at Darrix. He probably could, by all rights, kill him right now.

But Tomin chose not to. He chuckled instead. 'You are stubborn, I will give you that! I meant what I said; you'd make a fine paladin of Serros one day.'

'Thank you.'

'There are so few,' Tomin went on, 'that have the right blend of talents – devotion, faith, strength of arm. You have displayed them all! I would be surprised if that wasn't your calling, actually.'

Darrix smiled. 'You know as well as I do that we are supposed to take after the occupation of our parents in this land. It is a great dishonour to not obey them and to not … be like them.'

Kialessa knew what he was talking about; his strained relationship with his father. But Tomin probably wouldn't know any of that.

And so when the old warrior replied, he had no way of knowing how he was just convincing Darrix to dig in even more. 'No, not at all! It is true, most are born to be bakers or soldiers or farmers. But every once in a generation someone will be chosen from a city, or a town, to become a *hero*. Some are heroes for a day, some are heroes in their death. But some live a life of adventure and fame. You make a good point, this is not a "career" you choose, but a missive you accept from a higher power. If you, Darrix, are here to do great things, you **can** fight it, but it will not be to your salvation or happiness. I must simply insist you don't waste that calling on a fool's mission!'

Kialessa could see he was sure he'd convinced them to quit. Only when he saw Darrix's expression did Tomin seem to realise he'd just given him motivation to continue doing just what he was doing.

A life of slaying dragons or saving kings wasn't a "job" one chose. But when one chose to stand up for what they believed, well, it would define forever in the minds of others who they were.

Darrix would never be the paladin Tomin wanted.

And then Tomin burst out laughing. It seemed to chase away any lingering fear and doubt, any indication that he would physically rip the pole down with his bare hands if he wanted to. He looked at them, a twinkle in his eye. Then, in a miracle in itself, he bowed to Darrix, and even nodded to her. Still laughing he turned, hefting his sword over one shoulder and walked out, his posk following along without any visible cue.

Kialessa wasn't sure what had just happened, but she laughed too.

'He leaves this situation to a power higher than himself,' Darrix explained.

The paladin's hearty laugh echoed around the broken shrine as he walked away.

     By Dr Joseph Ireland "Dr Joe"

***

An hour later, Darrix's father returned with a cleric of Serros in tow, one of the retinue of the High King's messenger. 'Ahh, now, m'boy, let's see what you have to say against a *legal* messenger of the gods now, eh?'

Darrix scowled but the cleric spoke kindly. 'Please, don't antagonise the youth further. If I may speak to your son?'

'Knock yourself out.' He stood by the wall, arms folded.

The cleric shook his head patiently, but grew sadder as he looked on Darrix, tied to a pillar.

'It should not have come to this,' the old cleric said. 'This was not the unity the High King sought to bring among the people.'

'Are they doing this to the elves as well? How about the dwarven deities?'

'No, the dwarves worship the old Pantheon already, though they once gave them different names. The elves too –'

'So it is religious oppression all around?' Darrix said, his voice mocking. 'What is it that you hope to achieve? Do you really think you can make a people forget their beliefs?'

The cleric looked at him condescendingly, 'I haven't

come here to argue with you, boy. The old Pantheon are the only good gods, all else are flawed.'

'How can you say that?' Kialessa asked. 'They fight among themselves just as much as any of us, except they hurl forests when they do. What about when Pumos put a bunch of rotten fish outside Serros' front door?'

Darrix smiled. 'Or the great feast in honour of the Overgods that eventually resulted in the birth of evil – no fault of Mya's, I'm told.'

The cleric was trying to hide his anger. 'We are to consider such events as analogies for the real deeds of the gods that go beyond our mortal comprehension.'

'That they do,' Kialessa muttered.

He looked down at her in disgust, but Kialessa was used to seeing that attitude when people looked at her.

'And what of your god, Darrix? Why would he have you tie yourself to a pole?' The cleric asked.

'Sometimes, He would not. I know the gods are sometimes hard to find, and even harder to comprehend. But there is one more important difference between your gods and mine. The Eternal does not need our faith. He is not like the Old gods. They need us to believe in them to be strong. But the Eternal just seeks for us to know Him because he wants to, because He **loves** us.'

The cleric seemed to take pity on Darrix and put a hand kindly on his shoulder. 'In the war of the gods, Neth grows stronger with every thought, word or deed that denies the old Pantheon. I am not supposed to tell you, but in the coming days and seasons, everything, *everything*, will depend on our unity and the strength of the Old gods. You **must** worship them boy, for this deed brings them sorrow and weakens their strength –'

'If anything weakens the true gods of goodness it will **not** be failing to call on them,' Darrix argued. 'It will be the acts of evil, of lying and deception, cruelty and injustice. Just the kind of injustice the High King is enacting by bringing out his false and hypocritical laws!'

'Now watch your tone with me, boy!' The cleric replied. 'I am a righteous cleric of the Old faith, and Serros is my light. Your Eternal will be put back into the darkness shortly, where all can see his value.'

It took a moment for Darrix to calm down. 'Sorry, your honour, but I must disagree. The Eternal is a god of good. If you ever overcame your fear, you would know this if you visited our shrine, if you came and sought goodness sincerely. No god of goodness would deceive you. Why not visit?'

The cleric calmed down too. 'If there is any goodness in your Eternal, and he is true, then it is because he is only a shadow, a memory, of the Overdeity Halm.'

Darrix smiled. 'Halm is taught by your *own faith* to be uncaring. The Eternal **is** love and has paid the price of our weaknesses to show us He cares and seeks relationship with each of us.'

'And where does this god come from?'

'I am not told. Another world, perhaps? We do not know all we need to, just enough to begin our journey of faith. A journey I will not end for you, for even the High King, till I stand in the presence of my god and thank Him. I will not give up the truth I have found, not even for Serros, not even for all the gods of the old Pantheon combined.'

The cleric grew dark once more. 'Then you are lost to us. Stay here in your darkness. There is nothing more I can do here.' He stalked off.

For a long time there was silence. Then, glaring at Kialessa, Darrix's father walked up to him and struck him on the face.

The two men looked at each other. Lost for words, Darrix's father left.

Kialessa and Darrix were both silent in the fading light, while she helped dry his silent tears with the hem of her college shirt.

Whispers of despair

Know when to quit. Know when you have gone far enough, know when another step will do more harm than good. Know when to quit.

– Elven Queensage of the North – Sagesse L'aimé.

Piex returned late that evening full of excitement, just as the sun was turning the sky a brilliant orange. Kialessa was starving, but Darrix didn't even seem to be a bit distressed or hungry anymore. Allastassia arrived a moment later, eager to share news of the further destruction the High King's men were wreaking on King

Dunnkan's people. Even Posk was there, looking nervous and acting cautious.

Piex couldn't wait to share his news. 'They like it,' he said. 'They're putting together a case right now and are planning to take it to the High King in the morning. The High King might have made a mess here, but if they can stop him from disrupting the other kingdoms …'

'Then this is good!' Kialessa said. 'Perhaps you should go with them?' she asked Darrix.

'No, I'm staying here till the law changes.'

'If you want,' Allastassia said, her voice soft and diplomatic, 'but I think you've already made a powerful point. News of the High King's attack on King Dunnkan's "rebellion" has already spread to neighbouring kingdoms and everywhere that news goes, they tell about the young boy who stood two days chained to a circle of the Eternal. Perhaps you can do more good carrying these issues to the High King himself?'

'It's not like they invited me,' he argued.

'What, the circle?' Piex began, seeming a little unsure of what was being talked about, 'I don't think Darrix could carry-'

'Actually, that's a great idea Piex!' Darrix said. 'Tell them I'll cut myself down from this place only when I have King Dunnkan's word that I can carry this circle in person to the High King's palace.'

'I don't think that's actually a good –' Kialessa began.

'But it's huge!' Allastassia cut in.

'Wait, what? No, that's not what I was suggesting!' Piex complained.

'Please ask…' Allastassia said to Piex, clearly eager to have Darrix unshackled at any cost.

Piex thought about that, then said to Allastassia, 'It might help if you came. You can get people to agree to anything.'

'I'd not be too sure of that if I were you,' Allastassia mumbled, but she went with Piex anyway.

Darrix breathed deeply. 'Two days is a long time to be strung up. My arms stopped hurting a long time ago.' His voice trailed off as they heard someone approaching, the sharp and crisp footsteps echoing in the vacant courtyard made her feel nervous. Posk growled.

It was the third messenger.

When he spoke, it was with a condescending tone. 'Oh, so it's the brave, foolish boy who's tied himself to a pole in a vain attempt at usurping true gods with his own made up one.'

They said nothing.

'You really think the High King is going to care one bit about a little teenager who's tied himself up to a pole somewhere near the edge of his kingdom? Hundreds of thousands of people depend on him every day for the difference between life and death. What do you honestly think you can do?'

'Be silent,' Darrix ordered.

Posk interposed himself between them.

'You're a waste of time and a waste of breath,' the messenger hissed, 'and your life doesn't matter. When you've starved to death at that pole, they'll cut your lifeless husk down and burn it on that pole you've died to protect. No one will remember you or the cause you've died for.'

'You've just made a big mistake,' Darrix said darkly, 'because now I know you're *frightened* of me making just such a sacrifice. I'll stay on this circle till I die or the High King changes his law!'

The messenger did not look surprised but actually rather pleased. 'Well, it's a good thing that you can always depend on a paladin to keep their promise.'

Darrix just smiled darkly in return, but as Kialessa watched, the golden flame died from the circle.

***

The others were surprised when they returned. They'd even brought Allastassia's house priest to try and heal some of the swelling in Darrix's wrists. But he refused to leave. Allastassia again begged him tearfully but he would not even take a little food and water.

'Be swift,' he said, 'I can hold on another two weeks, maybe more. I'm getting used to it.'

'But your body is not,' Allastassia's mother said. 'Already I hear an illness at your chest. I think the time has come where it is wisdom that you leave –'

'I WILL NOT!' Darrix shouted.

Yet Kialessa could tell Lady Annadaria was right, he was becoming unwell. The messenger's words had left him angry and though everyone told him to, no one could make him leave that pillar.

'Darrix,' Piex began. 'I can foresee some complications …'

'Not you as well.' Darrix complained, so Piex held his peace.

No one argued with Darrix then, and one by one, they all left. They had a court case to go to. But Kialessa had nowhere to go. So she just stayed and helped him wait.

***

By late afternoon on the third day it was raining. The mission to the High King had already left, and few came to see the tae'anaryn and the boy on the pillar. The wind was cold as it drifted lazily through the open area where the shrine once stood. Darrix was exhausted beyond his mortal strength, and lay quietly at the pillar's base as though he'd gladly wished someone would cut him away.

The day had been painfully long since the messenger's spiteful visit. Then, as they watched the sun move across the sky, Darrix had started to cough. Now he suffered regular coughing fits as some terrible illness worked its way through his body.

Now, the sun long set in the fading evening, Kialessa was the only one keeping watch, cuddled as best she could next to Darrix, trying to protect them both from the cold. Darrix, too, had noticed the loss of the golden flame and took it to mean the presence of the Eternal had withdrawn, but it had not returned.

Kialessa didn't dare ask what it meant. Was this a test? Or was this the Eternal's way of telling them to cease their vigil and move on? She did not know, and Darrix didn't mention it.

There were footsteps now, soft ones, of an adult making his way towards the darkened area. After a moment she could see Darrix's father approaching across the broken stone, carrying a magical lantern. She roused Darrix, who appeared to be either sleeping or passed out. It was quite an effort to wake him.

'Son …' the older man began in a husky voice, as though he'd done nothing but cry all day.

For a long time there was silence. Then he began again, 'Son. I think it's time to come home.'

'No,' Darrix insisted, his voice thin but determined.

'Darn you, son! Can't you see this is killing you? What good are you to your cause like this?'

Darrix didn't answer at first. 'Funny to hear you

mention my beliefs,' he muttered.

But Darrix's father didn't seem interested in getting into an argument. 'I need you home, boy. Your mother is worried sick and I … I need you home, son.'

Darrix adjusted his position so he sat up a little more and gave his father a kind smile. 'I have to stay,' he began, and Kialessa was surprised to hear the edge of tears to his voice now as well. 'Don't you see? I *have* to.'

His father did not argue. 'I wanted so *much* for you,' he said, quietly, looking up toward the stars. 'I've two children already in the military. If you didn't take to business, I thought you could at least take to the army like them. But you're not like them at all. You always were … determined. You see things differently. I must say, I don't understand you at all, but I do know that nothing I do can stop you from becoming what you choose to be. I see that now and that … that's not a very easy thing for a father to accept, my boy.'

Darrix smiled.

'You know,' his father continued, 'I even tried to get King Dunnkan to order you from that stupid pole but he refused. You know this will kill you, don't you, son? Before the week's end if not tonight?'

The father stifled a sob, then spoke to Kialessa. 'You … you're a good friend to him, aren't you young gentle, K… oh, I still forget your name. You … you'll watch over my son, won't you?'

She nodded, not sure of what he was asking for and not sure why he was asking it.

Then the great merchant, more than six feet of muscled, burly man, bent down and suddenly wept great tears of sadness on his resolute young son's head. 'If it's *that* important to you, my boy, what can I or your mother, do against it? I can't agree with what you're doing, but I might as well move a mountain with my bare hands as stand in the way of it. So if anyone can take you from your wretched pillar, it's all up to Him now. I'm going to ignore the High King's law tonight, and talk to this Eternal of yours. If you live to see the morning … well, that would mean the world to me.'

While he spoke, a small fleck of white fire burnt in his hands, and then he pressed them together as though he might pray. The fire stayed there till he touched his hands to his son's shoulders, and the flames absorbed into Darrix. Both men acted as if they didn't see anything at all.

'I have to leave,' his father said. He walked quickly into the night, his huge shoulders trembling as he was unable to contain his sobs further.

Again, they were alone once more.

'Perhaps …' Darrix began, but stopped suddenly. 'No. This might be the hard way but it's the way I choose. I will see it through to the end like this. They need to know and I will show them.'

     By Dr Joseph Ireland "Dr Joe"

'Why Darrix?'

'Because this is what I choose.'

Kialessa snuggled next to him. 'Then I suppose not even the Eternal will take that choice away from you.'

***

Most of the night went by in miserable dark and the soft rain did not stop. Kialessa finally stumbled to her feet to stretch the aching pain in her back and legs, but knew it would be nothing to the agony Darrix would be feeling, as he could no longer stand at all. She turned and watched him lying slumped, still chained, at the wooden pillar. His hair was a shamble of knots and he didn't seem to be breathing.

She walked up to him, stumbling through the clods of dirt and broken ground that was once a sacred shrine. She could no longer contain her tears. Would nothing free him?

He stirred as she approached but she stopped when she saw his eyes, bloodshot and angry. It looked like his soul had left him. He said nothing and showed no happiness at her presence like he used to.

'Darrix, I …' Kialessa began, but found she had no words to say.

He shut his eyes and bent his head forwards. 'I don't feel Him anymore.'

'Who?'

'The presence of the Eternal. It's like I'm in the night. I've always been close but now … I don't know what's happened.'

'The fire …' she began. 'I haven't seen it all day. Not since the messenger … Maybe it's time to, you know …'

At the mention of the messenger's name Darrix grew angry. 'No! **Don't** tell me what to do! You're *just* like the rest of them!'

She burst into tears. 'Darrix, you can't stay like this! You'll die! I can't let you die. I … I'm your friend.'

But he just stared at her, his eyes dark pools of anger and betrayal. 'If the Eternal decides I have to end this journey alone, then so be it.'

Kialessa burst into tears again but she would not leave him. So she sat there on her heels in the mud, in the rain, and helped him mourn.

And that was how they found her, two hours later, after Darrix had called them. She'd fallen forwards, too weak and cold to rise, unaware of how the water had almost covered her mouth. They picked her up without a word, though she'd tried to tell them she wanted to stay. Then she'd fainted again and could say nothing as they carried her inside. She was only briefly aware of someone helping change her wet clothes, of someone drying her wrinkled and cold skin, of someone tucking her into the softest, warmest bed she'd ever been in.

       By Dr Joseph Ireland "Dr Joe"

9 At the pillar

Then she drifted into a fervid sleep of silent nightmares.

***

Kialessa knew them now. They were horses. They didn't seem to be able to see her hiding there in the shadows, or if they did, they didn't care. There were hundreds of them in perfect rows, red sparks thrown up from the cobblestones of a broken city. She pressed herself against the shadows of the arch where she hid.

She had returned to the dream. She had a vague sense of someone being there with her, guiding her, but it was not anyone she could see.

Then another presence found her and a cruel voice whispered by her ear, *I told you so...*

She gasped but did not flee. She knew who it was – the hooded demon. It began to sing a familiar poem in a child's voice, the words perverted and all wrong;

'Four sets of four; birds in a pie,
Nothing left, but for them to cry,
Watch it as their throats run dry,
Time, little child, for them all to die...'

'It's not over yet,' she promised.

It will be soon, it crooned in a tarrying whisper. *With each curse I grow stronger, with every misery we gain ground. You've done well, little one. Soon this whole nation will be brought to ashes, and given over to my master.*

Kialessa watched the black horses, their dark hooves thundering on the pavement. It was as if their number had grown, obscuring their forces with the dust and darkness their footprints threw into the air.

Soon, it will be enough, the malevolent voice whispered.

          By Dr Joseph Ireland "Dr Joe"

She suddenly recognised magic in its words, powerful words of despair and hopelessness. He was trying to weaken her.

She fought desperately for the words to fight it. 'All? No, there will always be power to resist.'

It laughed, trying to spin her around with mocking sounds. It appeared to be unable or unwilling to touch her. *All,* it repeated. *Even **he** approaches me now and there is nothing you can do to stop it!*

There was a loud crack as the horses' hooves struck the pavement and the ground split. At the far end of the street Kialessa saw a young man. A horse reared up in front of him, very much like the day she'd first seen Mask.

The boy fell backwards into the crevasse of fire, only barely holding on with a single hand. His helmet slipped off and Kialessa saw immediately who it was.

'Darrix!' she screamed.

She ran across the street, horses pulling back to let her pass. The mocking laughter dragged at her mind, weakening her limbs. At the last instant she threw herself on the ground and clutched onto Darrix's hand.

'Darrix, hold on to me!' she plead.

But his hand was weak. She looked over the edge and in his eyes. They were bloodshot, broken. He looked angry and tired.

'Why?' he said with a bitter voice. 'What's the point?'

Wrenching his hand away from her he plunged

towards the fiery abyss, thrashing about violently as he fell.

It was only a dream, but she knew something terrible was about to happen…

Kialessa screamed.

Confrontation

If you really believe your god is all powerful, then you also believe he could have stopped this from happening. But he didn't. So either he doesn't care… or perhaps he cares so much that he chose to let it happen for better reasons than you can currently comprehend.

– Jacinthia, High priestess of the Eternal, castle records 15.2.313.

Once again, the shattering sound that was her scream woke the entire castle. Then Kialessa shouted, 'Darrix is in terrible danger!'

The two nearby nurses had covered their ears and thrown themselves away from her. Kialessa saw she was in the little medical house the king kept at his castle.

Awake and filled with energy, she was up on her feet and searched for her magical sash. Gratefully, it was close by. Having magic clothes was a great advantage in an emergency, and as soon as it was on her, the soft leather armour folder itself around, her whip curling out from its enchanted hiding place.

'What are you talking about, child?' The head nurse asked.

'Darrix is in danger!'

'He's in the broken shrine –'

'No he's not,' she said, somehow knowing. 'He's going to see the messenger!'

Kialessa ran across the ground, only dimly aware of the strangeness of it all. It was day and she was running to save Darrix from the danger he was in. In her mind's eye she saw him, by the third messenger's door, knocking out the guards with unholy strength. There was darkness all around him and his eyes were filled with a cold, murderous bloodlust. It was a dream but she had seen it, and was sure it was true.

If she didn't stop him, there was no telling what he'd do.

Kialessa raced to the messenger's door and gasped when she saw them. Two of the king's guard, adults, both knocked senseless and unconscious as though by an armoured thug, or a boy driven mad. How he'd managed to defeat two adults …

… It had happened somehow. Darrix had gone insane.

She heard a groan; one of the guards was still alive. Her heart leapt within her – he hadn't killed them! Perhaps there was still good in him? Perhaps if she could reach that?

He'd be on his way to the royal guest room now. Only a few rooms away. She knew had to cut him off. She didn't wait to catch up to him but leapt straight out of the window, and running right along the edge without stopping or pausing, jumped back in at the top of the stairs that led towards the guest chambers.

He was there.

She saw a light around him then, just for a moment. It was as though it was made of the thickest black. His father's sword was held limply in his hand but she knew from experience he could flick it to life at any moment. The pommel of that sword was tinged with the blood of all those who'd been in his way. His clothes were tattered and torn but he didn't have a single wound on him. His hair was wild and his eyes devoid of hope, and he had a look of dark anger around him. It was more frightening than facing down an archmage.

He was planning revenge.

He was planning on murdering the messenger.

He looked at her. In that moment, she realised she would die before she let him throw his life away on a senseless murder.

'Not like this,' she said.

'You know *nothing!*' he hissed in a bitter voice that didn't seem his own. 'I have been betrayed. I have been abandoned by my god. There is nothing left for me in the world!'

'Not like this.'

'Get out of my way!' He raised his sword and prepared to rush at her.

Perhaps she was afraid of him, or afraid for him, but with a movement faster than she knew she was capable of she swung her whip out at him and struck him full force on the back of his sword hand.

With a cry, he dropped his sword, his hand bleeding from the enormous bruise she'd just given him. He fell to his knees beside the little stone drinking fountain there. 'You! I'll cut you! I'll … I'll …' And his tears began to flow freely for the first time.

'I can't let you,' she said, as her own tears made it impossible for her to see him clearly. 'I am your friend.'

He left the sword where it lay and wept freely.

Slowly, carefully, she came down to where he sat and put her hand on his shoulder. He might have considered pushing her aside but was too weak from illness and sorrow. Instead, like a trembling child, he put his head on her shoulder and cried.

She reached to the fountain, and drawing water in a cup gave him some to drink. He must have been parched, yet drank little. He drew some water across the welt on his hand, but nothing changed.

'Were I pure before the Eternal,' he muttered, 'this wound would be healed already.'

'I know.'

It seemed like eternity. But then he nodded.

Somehow she'd stopped him. Or rather since he was quite a bit stronger than she was, she'd managed to help him stop himself.

'You were the only one that stayed Kialessa,' he said. 'I could **never** hurt you.'

He looked in her eyes and smiled, and slowly she saw the light of hope returning. 'Oh!' he continued, 'I've much to atone for. I knocked out five guards, oh! Why did the Eternal abandon me at the pillar? I only wanted to serve him to the end with everything, but …'

She had no idea what to say, and so said nothing.

Eventually he smiled through his tears and spoke again. 'You are right, Kialessa. Murder … this is not the right way. I do not know what is, but I do accept that.' He coughed, deeply and painfully. With alarm, Kialessa saw a speck of blood curl out upon his lips.

Darrix continued, 'I don't know why … I can't see why He'd do this, why he'd let His shrine be defiled and His people imprisoned for believing in Him. I don't know why, but if this is how it must be done, then … this is the way it *will* be done. I'll let it all happen, even if I can't see why it's the right thing to do. Thank you, Kialessa, for reminding me of that. Thank you for having the courage to tell me … to stop doing what I knew was wrong.'

With his words of faith, she saw a white fire flood from the roof and brush away all the darkness. He didn't seem to notice but he breathed in deeply, though his chest still rattled with illness.

'That,' said Kialessa, 'sounds like a *good* choice.'

They smiled at each other, and Kialessa sighed.

That was a little easier than I thought, she wondered, her heart filling with hope once more.

Suddenly the door at the top of the stairs where she had just been burst violently open. Kialessa gasped in surprise while Darrix slowly and painfully reached out to grasp the hilt of his sword again.

Almost leisurely, a terrible sense of wilful evil begun to ooze down the stairs. A shadowy figure appeared at the top, radiating that evil presence.

It was the third messenger.

'Oh, poor, young fools!' he boasted. 'It would have made things much more believable if you'd just let that boy attack me in my room! But I suppose it'll do if the battle takes place here.'

'What?' Darrix demanded.

The messenger swiftly raised one hand, holding the rod the second messenger had wielded, and spoke a word at them. A terrible confusion filled Kialessa's mind and chilled her bones, and try as she might, she could not resist the paralysis that suddenly overtook her.

'I do not have the strength to paralyse you too, yet boy,' the Messenger said, 'but after I kill you, in "self-defence", they'll find it was your sword that slew her, and I will tell them in your madness you cut her down as well.'

Darrix was silent.

Kialessa could hardly see him.

'This was all your plan? From the beginning?' Darrix said.

The messenger took a step toward them, but Darrix did not flinch.

'I see now,' Darrix said. 'You wanted me to attack you. I'd been told it was enough, I was ready to leave that pillar, but then you came and provoked me. So I ignored His will until I lost hope. You knew I would do it, and then you would kill me ... but Kialessa stopped me, and now you plan to kill us both and blame it on me!'

The messenger smiled. 'If you need it in so much detail, sure. But it will not matter and no one will care, once they see how a servant of the Eternal attempted to murder the High King's messenger! Make your peace boy.'

'You'll not find me so easy to defeat now that my hope is restored!'

The messenger laughed, a truly wicked sound, though in the new light he looked thin and afraid. Through the faith of whatever evil deity sustained him he called down another prayer at Darrix – a wave of fear. But Darrix simply smiled.

The messenger looked surprised.

'I fell right into your plan!' Darrix shook his head, voice full of indignation. He stood up slowly. 'He told me, you know. Advised me to leave you to your evil, to take up the circle and leave. But I ignored His council. I thought He left me. But in truth, I left Him. Now I repent. Now I return.'

'And now you will die,' the messenger said and began to pray again.

'For the Eternal!' Darrix shouted, and in that great shout Kialessa found the paralysing powers fail around her. With long strides, Darrix ran right into the messenger and pushed him back into the room at the top of the stairs. The messenger managed to block Darrix's sword with his own sharp dagger but his wicked prayer was lost as the young boy, who was taller than he, punched him hard in the chest.

Kialessa rushed up the stairs after them. The room beyond was not what it should be. The sense of evil was tangible there. A great circle was inscribed into the floor and around it several marks of the Pantheon were written, but they were all wrong. And once more at the head, where Serros should have been, another strange and wicked symbol lay.

 By Dr Joseph Ireland "Dr Joe"

Darrix was in the centre of that circle and the messenger, unaware that Kialessa had broken his prayer, and seemingly convinced that he wasn't in any danger in King Dunnkan's castle, stood with his back facing towards her. 'That trick has only won you a moment's grace, boy,' he jeered. 'Now you are in my domain like a fly in a spider's web. My master will have you.'

'Who is your master?!' Darrix demanded.

'You'll know soon enough,' the messenger crooned and a dark purple nimbus of light begun to gather around him. 'The only creator here is mine …'

But Darrix stood confidently, 'Not so – the Eternal is a power omnipresent. There is no place His light is not. I command your wickedness to leave, by the Eternal's light!'

It was a battle of faith. Darrix tried to dispel the gathering darkness with light, while the evil messenger tried to summon something into the circle or force Darrix out of it into who knows what unholy dimension. Kialessa crept silently into the room, by the door, where the messenger could not see her, ready to act at the most opportune moment.

With a sudden gust of wind that swept out from the air above Darrix, the dark light scattered. He lowered his sword threateningly. 'You are no messenger of the High Kingdom, but are a servant of Neth or Pumos, no doubt. You're not trying to advance the old Pantheon at all, but to imprison the people with your twisted faith! I'm beginning to think the war has already begun, and the first war is against the freedom to choose what you believe in. I think you're after the faith in the Eternal!'

The messenger looked angry. 'You're too clever to keep alive another moment.' He lifted an unholy symbol from his robes and held it out towards Darrix. The boy charged the messenger but Kialessa was faster.

As silent as a cat, she leapt up and wrapped her whip around the man's thin throat and pulled hard. His hand raced up to it just as Darrix struck the unholy symbol from his other hand and threw him to the floor. He struggled with surprising strength, held down only by Darrix's renewed power and indomitable faith.

'Hold him still!' Darrix said.

'I can't. There's something not right here. He's too strong!' Kialessa said.

Darrix looked down at her, and she realised her eyes were glowing in excitement and fear.

A look of understanding crossed Darrix's face. He, too, understood now that the messenger was not only working for, but was being controlled by, a demon.

And that, fortunately, was something the priests of the Eternal were noted for handling with great efficiency.

'By the Eternal!' Darrix shouted and pointed down at the man's heart a prayer of exorcism, speaking to the evil spirit, and not the messenger. 'Come out of him! Let him go!'

What happened next was a sight Kialessa hoped never to see again. A grey mist of darkness began to exude from the messenger, who lay silently on the floor. The darkness formed the shape of a man with a mist for legs. The full measure of evil that exuded from it weakened them, and Kialessa trembled at its open rebellion against all that was good.

'Very good, young boy,' it said with all the distain and arrogance that the messenger had used, yet with a voice so soft it was almost a whisper. 'You have brought me out of my slave here. Perhaps you **are** a threat worthy of the master's notice.'

'Wisp demon,' Darrix uttered, seeming to be able to say no more.

The demon then turned towards Kialessa, spinning in the air around her. It swayed and danced as it spoke, as if toying with her, or perhaps trying to find a weakness in her spirit it could exploit, 'and **why** am I not surprised to find you here, little tae'anaryn? I knew you would ignore my warning, so it was a simple matter to convince you to go wandering on a pleasant day, alone in your familiar woods. Such an easy matter to convince a drake to hunt you, once it had found your scent. What a *pity* the protector had a protector herself, or your death that day might have saved you from the agony I will bring upon you and your loved ones now!!'

It moved to touch her shoulder, but its form suddenly shimmered as Darrix swept up his sword through the ghostly creature, passing straight through. Darrix stood back, showing no sign of fear.

The demon hissed a whispered laugh, 'None of your weapons can harm this body, nor can your armour protect you from my touch.'

It reached out to Darrix, who dodged sideways.

'No ...' the messenger husked painfully from the floor. Thorn bushes of dark light suddenly sprang up, keeping Darrix and herself away.

The wisp demon turned to looked down at the fallen messenger. 'Don't even try to resist me now, mortal. You are mine by our oath.'

'I never...!' The messenger's words stumbled among themselves, 'I didn't know you would ... You deceived me, leave!'

It looked almost sad. 'So now you choose to die too?' It reached down to the man with deliberate, tormenting leisure even as the shards began to dissipate. Darrix tried to grab the demon, but pulled his hand back in pain.

'Oh Eternal ...' Kialessa whispered, knowing it would come for them both next.

Footsteps echoed out in the stairs, and the old dwarven priestess rounded the doorway. It was Jacinthia, priestess of the shrine of the Eternal, dressed like a gardener, a piece of grass twisted into a circle emitting

      By Dr Joseph Ireland "Dr Joe"

brilliant white light. She held out her home-made symbol of faith.

'Eternal's light,' she whispered. As Kialessa watched, a beam of light as bright as a sun shot past her and right into the evil spirit's chest. It roared in surprise and pain, momentarily stunned by the brilliant energy.

Another adult human reached the doorway and pushed past the priestess in such a hurry it almost knocked her flat.

It was Tomin, the paladin of Serros.

'Here, boy!' he shouted, tossing a sword to Darrix, who caught Defender and grasped it in both hands.

'Demon spawn!' the paladin roared. The evil spirit hardly had time to look up from the blast of light it had received from the priestess when the mighty paladin charged it. Shrieking, it left the messenger trembling on the floor and took flight towards the window. It shattered them with a bitter swipe of its tendrilous claws and escaped into the alley beyond.

'Get it, before it escapes!' Tomin shouted. He was looking towards the priestess, but Darrix had already taken action.

The young man leapt through the broken window, and without pausing, ran along the ground at full speed. He seemed so much faster than should have been possible for someone who'd been fasting for three days.

Yet the wisp demon was even faster. It kept to the

shadows, clearly looking for a way to escape. The semi-physical being collided with the ground and bounced away, then crashed into the castle keep and fell back with a hellish screech. Seeing Darrix, it turned and headed for the alley exit at the far end, where a town fountain flowed.

'Slay it!' the priestess told him in a surprisingly loud whisper. 'Its form must be destroyed in this world or it will continue to tempt others.'

There was a piercing whistle from Darrix, and an instant later, the thunder of hooves could be heard. Mask rounded the corner let out a terrifying battle cry. Mask reared up, his hooves bursting out with white fire as Tomin muttered a prayer, the light so bright it was visible for all to see.

The demon reared back in horror, momentarily paralysed by surprise or fear.

Without pausing for breath, Darrix leapt up. The creature spun around with supernatural speed, but Defender twisted sideways to deflect the blow. Then Darrix, with a mighty roar, brought the blade down on the demon and sundered the creature from its skull to its wispy end.

With a sigh, it dissipated. In that moment it seemed almost all the fear and oppression in the castle fled, perhaps even in the entire kingdom.

Darrix turned and smiled grimly at them, Mask walked up, and he embraced him, leaning heavily. He

     By Dr Joseph Ireland "Dr Joe"

looked almost too exhausted to stand.

And Tomin, leaning on his sword as though he had all the time in the world, was laughing loud enough for the entire castle to hear. 'You did it, boy! You brought low a *demon*! At your age, ha! I **told** you that you were made to be a **hero**!'

Then Kialessa heard a man crying from the floor. It was the messenger, having been hauled to his feet by an angry and powerful high priestess. When he spoke, his voice was high and whiney, as you might expect from the small human he was. It was not the arrogant and confident voice of the demon that possessed him and that had ordered the gods of the people's choice be removed. 'What have I done? I'm so sorry. What have I done?'

'Khen Pawl,' Tomin said, 'you are under arrest for consorting with evil spirits, for bringing chaos to the High Kingdom, and counselling the High King with your treachery!'

The messenger paled. 'My fate is terrible.' Then he looked out at Darrix. 'He stood up to him. He stood up to him when I never could. How …'

The messenger fell to weeping as other royal guards arrived. Moments later, he was led out in chains while Tomin made an account to all the officials, both King Dunnkan's men and the Royal Guard of the High King.

The paladin's squire

Honour, praise, wealth; all pale in comparison to the clear conscience of an honest person.

– Lumos, goddess of time, to King Erell after the battle of Aurem fields.

Thunder rumbled in a clear blue sky and an intense peace settled through the broken shrine; a sure sign that the watchful presence of the gods drew nigh.

Kialessa couldn't keep the tears of gratitude from her eyes, but this was a good time to cry. They were in the new shrine, not even completed yet. It was still open to

   By Dr Joseph Ireland "Dr Joe"

the sky above, but the pillar to the Eternal, the one some now called Darrix's Pillar, stood where it always had. Before it, a course, rough wagon carriage box had been turned on its side to make a temporary altar. Someone's torn cloak was lain across it with great respect, softening its splintered appearance. But most importantly, there was now only one shrine. There were no longer two, for the royals and the people. One shrine, for all people.

'It is amazing,' Darrix said. He was sitting next to Kialessa in the front row by his four closest friends. He was dressed in the formal armour his father had fitted for him just that morning.

Kialessa turned to look at him while they waited.

He looked up at the pillar, towards the glory he alone could see there. He continued, 'It's amazing what the priests of faith can do on this world. I wish everyone could see what their faith can do. Look closely, Kialessa. Perhaps you will see what is *really* happening when people sincerely believe in a thing that is good and right.'

Between the pillar and the alter the king rose to speak. 'We are here today to honour a young man whose bold courage and conviction has freed us all from the tyranny of oppression. Darrix Minerson, third child born to Harrobar and Niania Minerson. Rise and receive your honour.'

Darrix breathed in. He seemed uncomfortable in the formal armour. But he stood and knelt at the altar before his God and his king.

King Dunnkan smiled. 'Were it requisite, I would grant you title in my kingdom and lands beyond your father's name. But I am only a king of men. Any reward befitting you today goes **beyond** my authority.'

King Dunnkan stood aside, a few people muttering their amazement at such humble words.

The priestess rose and spoke. 'Darrix, in vision I was shown all you have the potential to become. You are now called in His name to serve as a holy warrior, a paladin, the first to the Eternal. Do you accept it with all your heart?'

'I do.'

'Now, as you are the first, you are in need of training. A council has been held in the heavens regarding you, as it is often for us all. Know this, Darrix; one has been chosen to be your guide, your teacher, and your trainer.'

He smiled up at her and she smiled back. Then she stood aside.

All gasped when Tomin, paladin of Serros, stood in authority between the pillar and the altar to a god that was not his. He grinned but still managed to look serious. 'It seems our gods may yet have need of their alliance, boy. I am chosen and take you willingly as my new squire.'

The people murmured their approval.

Tomin continued. 'I might not understand or accept

your faith, boy, but I do know how to build a warrior. So know this: I will work you hard. I will work you to the **bone**. I will train you till you learn to fear failing my expectations more than your enemies' blades. Do you accept me as your master?'

Darrix was silent, then smiled as though he knew something not even Tomin did, 'Gladly.'

Tomin smiled too. 'Then, Darrix, holy warrior of the Eternal, you are welcomed to my service. I call on the faith of the divine forces of goodness to grant my young, imperfect squire unfailing health that he might serve every day he has been given. For his courage, I ask that he be blessed so he may never know fear again. Let the grace of the divine protect him in every way if he walks in unfailing perfection before all the law he has been given. So let it be!'

The people repeated the amen, then Tomin continued, 'You are to take my blade, Defender – it has seen little use in my hand, a gift from a good king of my youth. Yet in your hand it has already sundered a demon and helped send it back to suffering where it belongs! This sword is true, double edged, to divide asunder both lies and sinew. Keep it well and it will keep you.'

Darrix looked surprised as he took the blade with trembling, silent hands. Kialessa wasn't sure if he was upset. But as soon as he looked up at Tomin, respect and gratitude written all over his face, her fears were relieved.

Tomin stood aside then and the priestess again stood forward. 'Then I bless you with an honest heart that will always know integrity. I bless you with a steady hand and strong arm in all your days, that will not fail you in any quest you undertake for righteousness. I bless you with eyes that see and a wisdom that will not depart from you, in discerning good from evil and lies from truth. If you do not turn from the path you set your feet to this day, you will not know weariness, as you are in the way your god has set before you. This is the first blessing of the Eternal upon you.'

'Thank you.'

Then she took a horn, filled with the oil of anointing, and poured it on Darrix's head while intoning her final blessings. Kialessa saw a gleaming light, blindingly pure, yet with such surreal beauty she was unwilling to look away. It flowed from the sky above, through the oil, and all throughout Darrix, making him glow. She looked around and it was clear almost no one could see the pure witness of the Eternal that enveloped him. She was almost sad for them, wondering what it would be like to be surrounded by such radiance, and completely unaware. Wondering if, perhaps, the divine was always this close and real to them all but people didn't notice.

Darrix stood and turned, raising his new sword. The Eternal may have been subtle, but Serros was always a willing show off. A bright pillar of yellow fire erupted

 By Dr Joseph Ireland "Dr Joe"

from the sky and roared down on Darrix, making his sword glow with a painfully bright light. People cried out and fell back, except Darrix, Tomin and the priestess.

For a moment there was simply admiration as the bright light wrote new words into the sword and adorned Darrix's armour with sacred scripture.

Then Tomin's voice thundered through the confusion, 'Soldiers, I give you: Darrix, holy warrior of Lenmer'el! Demonbane! Paladin in squire of The Eternal!'

The soldiers took their cue, and drawing their swords, bashed the pommels on shields or breastplates in a formal salute. 'Hail, squire Darrix!'

As the blinding light receded, Kialessa saw Darrix and was glad. She noticed he was not admiring his glowing sword or basking in the warriors' admiration. He was not smiling at his parents, nor looking for his friends. He looked up into the heavens, a trembling smile of pure thanks on his face, where he silently whispered one phrase towards the heavens as the tears flowed freely down his cheeks.

Thank you.

***

The next day, Kialessa sat with her closest friends by a roadside shrine, watching a small gathering. It was a mother, her aged father and a little girl. They were putting flowers around the little stick that they'd driven into the ground once more. A little stick that said: *To the goddess Theiss, may you watch over all travellers on this road and keep them safe, and keep our son and brother safe as you lead him to his rest. Till we meet again in Serros' Light.*

'They're coming,' Piex said, always keen-sighted. Kialessa turned, and watched in silence as over three hundred soldiers and one heavily chained and weeping prisoner filed past and back onto the road towards the docks, and then on to the High Kingdom. The soldiers ignored the widow as she renewed a silent roadside shrine to her departed son, the very shrine that they'd torn down not three days ago.

'Do you think they're embarrassed?' Kialessa asked.

'Probably not, they were just following orders,' Darrix replied.

'I have news,' Allastassia announced. 'My father was on the council that took the preliminary judgements of the messenger, and I overhead him talking about it to my uncle.'

'You mean the sleepy one?' Kialessa said.

'That's the one!' Allastassia winked. 'It turns out that this messenger was a reasonably unsuccessful member of the High King's court until last season. Then all of a sudden he began a meteoric rise in power. It turns out that he procured a book that might have had a little addition hidden in one of the covers – a scroll for contacting a wisp demon.'

'No!' Piex said. 'Who would be such a fool?'

'Clearly, the messenger Khen Pawl would,' Kialessa replied.

'One can but wonder,' Allastassia said in a conspiratorial tone, 'how it even came to be there...'

Kialessa found herself wondering if she was supposed to know the answer. But it seemed that, for now, no one did.

Then Piex shared news too. 'The legal counsel to the High King is all but cancelled. He has made a most notable backtrack of policy now it is public knowledge that his messenger was being used by a wisp demon.'

'And you know,' Allastassia added, 'word can spread pretty quickly when a castle wizard teleports right to the capital and begins broadcasting the news to everybody.'

They laughed and it made Kialessa smile. It must have been quite a scene to have seen the bookish sagemaster chastening the High King in his own castle about the whole incident. Kialessa would have loved to have been behind a tapestry that day!

She looked over at Darrix, who sat there quietly, 'And your family, your father … is he all right?'

'He cannot be kept silent!' Allastassia answered for him. 'A son that is not only going to become a warrior but also a priest – a paladin! He tells everyone he meets and hardly talks about anything else. I hear he's even making new swords to commemorate the occasion, being that he is now the largest armour smith in the city.'

Still Darrix said nothing but she could tell from his smile he was pleased.

'And yet, there's more!' Allastassia continued. 'Have you not heard, as a final reward, King Dunnkan has given Darrix a mount of his own to use: The royal Mask himself!'

'No!' Kialessa and Piex chorused. She could not believe it.

'Although,' Allastassia said with a playful look, 'it may have something to do with the fact that Mask will allow none other to ride him anyway, not even the king!'

Kialessa grinned at that irony.

Then she noticed Darrix straightening up, and the smile died from Allastassia's face. He struggled to his feet and stood at attention.

She turned and found herself face to face with an approaching warrior; Tomin, Paladin of Serros. He loomed above them all on his grey Posk, his glimmering armour terrifying in the morning sun.

'You have finished practicing the morning exercises I gave you already?' he said in a grim voice to Darrix.

'Yes honoured,' Darrix replied like a soldier.

'And your morning devotionals and care of the horse?'

'I rose early,' Darrix said, 'and was then asked by the

guard captain to assist in watching the rededication of this shrine.'

'Hmmm,' Tomin almost growled, without a smile.

Kialessa frowned. She could not imagine being tutored under such a demanding and thankless master. But she noticed the shadow of a grin under his dark beard. 'I will be back soon to check on your progress.'

Darrix nodded. 'Thank you, sir.'

Tomin looked towards the grieving family while they stared back with grim and unpleasant faces. He said nothing.

Then his gaze fell on Kialessa and his face lit up with a wry smile. 'I am impressed,' he said in a voice loud enough for everyone to hear. 'You are the first tae'anaryn I've ever met that I haven't had to kill!'

Kialessa was silent as he laughed as his own joke, her friends saying nothing. She watched with wariness as his smile vanished and his hand drifted meaningfully to his legendary sword, a powerful nimbus of light brightening about it as it did every time it was drawn.

'I am not ignorant,' he said, 'of the rumours surrounding you, young *dame*. Some say that you bewitched Darrix, as perhaps you did the king. Others are even so bold as to claim the demon was invited here by you; to gain the trust of a kingdom you hope to bring to ruin one day…'

Despite herself, Kialessa's mouth fell open as her heart

pricked in pain. After all she'd done, did they still not believe her?

'But I am not ignorant either,' Tomin continued, 'of what I myself have witnessed. I saw the way you battled that demon. I beheld the righteousness in your eyes as you tried to bring it low. I know for whose cause you fought this day. I will not yet say you've earned the title the king has given you, young Honoured, but I will say you have earned my trust, thus far, to any who enquire after you. However ...' He leaned forward in his saddle. 'If you ever have cause to serve evil, I will kill you myself.'

Allastassia gasped. Darrix looked furious. The others were yet silent.

Kialessa stood there speechless. For all her life she'd been used to dealing with people's prejudice. But what was she to say when she was personally threatened by one of the most powerful, influential and respected people in all the land? What was she to say when he'd literally promised to kill her if she ever did a bad thing?

The answer took a moment to bubble up inside, but when it did, she found she could speak it without fear. 'I hope you do.'

He was visibly shocked by her reply. Then a broad grin spread across his face and he burst out laughing. 'Good! We have an understanding then.' With a wry smile that betrayed he might actually learn to trust her, he saluted them and left.

     By Dr Joseph Ireland "Dr Joe"

She smiled and sat back.

Darrix said nothing. In all the commotion, almost everyone else had overlooked her contribution, though Darrix tried to tell them. He had pointed out that without her, he would be a murderer and probably have been killed. Without her, the High King's edict would not have been overturned within a day. That without Kialessa, they might not be free to choose who they worshipped this morning.

But Kialessa didn't mind, sitting in the warm sun, watching a families' memorial at a roadside shrine like the free people they were supposed to be. She was happy sitting beside her best friends in the whole world, especially Darrix, who was smiling at her the way only a friend can when you've helped saved his life.

Without asking her permission, he reached out and held her hand, and held it for a long time.

10 Darrix, the paladin's squire, and Mask, the King's mount

 By Dr Joseph Ireland "Dr Joe"

Appendix

Thoughts to ponder

The curse

What do you think is going on in this chapter? Who do you think the rider is?

On how to succeed in life and business

Darrix's father's advice: life is like cutting stone. What projects do you think are best achieved little by little, carefully chipping away at them, while keeping in mind the bigger picture?

On the other hand, what projects are like hunting – swiftly striking at a golden opportunity when it comes along?

The message

What command is the High King trying to impose on King Dunnkan's kingdom? Do you think it's right for others to say what we should believe in? What would you do if someone made a law to tell you what you can believe in?

Horses

How does Posk put himself in danger? Given that he would not have known any better, do you think someone else should have been in charge of his safety? What preparations should they have made to keep him and others safe with new animals around?

How does Darrix calm the horse? Do you think this would work with a real frenzied animal?

Of friends

In this chapter Posk manages to tame a mount of his very own, a drake (a kind of wingless dragon). How does he do it?

Do you think Kialessa should have let the dangerous animal drown, especially when it didn't know she had just saved it and it was hungry? What should you do if you meet an aggressive, wild animal while all alone?

A good day

Here the five friends meet and are able to spend some time together. Do you think they spend their time together wisely? Should they have studied together or is it sometimes more valuable to simply hang out as friends and have fun?

Why do you think Allastassia makes 'a speech out of it' when they return the king's horse to him?

The paladin

What do you think of the famous paladin, Tomin? Does he like Kialessa? Does he like Darrix?

What reasons does Tomin give for obeying the law? It is important to obey the law all the time?

Whispers

What does Tomin tell Darrix is coming?

Tomin advises Darrix to choose his friends carefully. Can friends influence us that much? Do you think Kialessa makes a good friend to Darrix, and why?

The rebellion of King Dunnkan

Why does King Dunnkan refuse to remove the roadside shrine? For what reason, do you think, does King Dunnkan refuse to remove a shrine to a god he doesn't even worship?

The army of the High King

In this chapter the High King's army comes along to force King Dunnkan's people to accept a law they haven't agreed to. Do you think the government can physically force people to obey a law? Are there times when this is appropriate?

What do you think about various people's response to the army?

The vigil

Why did Darrix tie himself to the pillar? Was this wise or crazy? According to you, what is the right way to protest against a law you don't agree with?

Have you ever found that, when you wanted to do something that was important to you, it was no effort even when others might have found it tedious?

What do you think about Allastassia's response to the religious persecution?

 By Dr Joseph Ireland "Dr Joe"

Vigil day two

When do you know it's time to quit? If a project 'isn't working', is it time to quit? Do you think some people quit important projects too early? Do you think some people go overboard and fail to quit soon enough?

The messenger here deliberately provokes Darrix, who becomes more stubborn even though a safer course of action has been offered. Why did the messenger do this? Do adversaries of a cause sometimes try to make their opponents do excessive or dangerous things in defence of their cause, just to make them appear stupid or dangerous?

Whispers of despair

In this chapter, the wisp demon contacts Kialessa to boast about its accomplishments. It tries to weaken her hope in an attempt to have her quit trying. Yet even in her dream Kialessa finds something to care about. Do you have a cause you feel is important? How do you find the courage to carry on when nothing seems to be going your way?

Confrontation

How does Kialessa stop Darrix? Or does she stop him at all?

Violence is rarely the solution but sometimes it can seem unavoidable. In this story, a cruel and evil demon tries to physically harm the heroes. Does Kialessa try to take on this situation alone, or does she call for help? What should you do if a situation looks like it is going to end up in violence?

The paladin's squire

In the conclusion to the story, we witness Darrix's new rise to power as a squire (student) of a famous paladin (a holy warrior). How should one react when given great honours? What is the purpose of gaining great power?

 By Dr Joseph Ireland "Dr Joe"

History of the world

– by Aimhirghin Muirín, gnome historian.

This is the true story of how it all began.

In the beginning the world was empty. Halm, the ageless Over-god of time, took pity on the unaware world. In an uncharacteristic gesture of kindness, he besought his wife Lallaellaia (*lal – layel - liah*), the ageless universe, to help him to send life upon the earth. (These two only are the timeless gods –they have no beginning and cannot have any end.) Together, they caused a star to fall to the sleeping world.

From the falling starburst the six elder gods. Lumos, goddess of the moon to govern times. Serros, the sun, to bring warmth and light to the world and from him Lumos borrows her light. Pumos, who took care of darkness and was a great friend from the beginning of Lumos. Waglah, goddess of the oceans, and finally, after a long time, the twins Animas and Planas, inseparable twin gods of all that live – animals and plants respectively.

For a long time there was peace. The gods joined together in creation and filling the world with life. After a time, the world itself awoke and became aware, and became Mya, goddess of the earth and daughter to Lallaellaia. In the process of time, Mya set four noble gods to govern the seasons, Winter, Spring, Summer and

Autumn. Lumos, not to be outdone, created the four noble gods of the day; Midnight, Midday and the young boy twins Twilight and Dawn. The others thought it a great wisdom and rejoiced in their works.

Waglah, for her part, was busy tending the creatures of the oceans. Soon they grew great in number and her waves began to reach up upon the face of Mya. Forever patient, Mya did not murmur. Serros, however, always fiery and quick to offence, took anger at her cause and chastened Waglah for her rudeness.

Rather than be intimidated, Waglah replied, 'Be chilled, 'tis not thine concern, for 'tis life I bring and surely Mya would speak if there was a problem.'

Well, there was, or there wasn't until Waglah denied Serros, who angrily beat upon the goddess with a fierce heat. Within the heat the oceans boiled and many creatures fled into the depth of the oceans never to return. Serros, to his surprise and horror, saw how the steam filled the air, only to fall in great sheets of rain upon the face of Mya, scarring her once smooth surface. To this day Serros and Waglah have not quite forgiven each other, and though occasionally there is peace, the storm clouds that cover their anger still fill the air and bring us rain. Sadly from this first fight was born the servant god – Pikal, the god of lightning, who lives only for strife and battle.

This, however, was not the birth of wickedness.

        By Dr Joseph Ireland "Dr Joe"

Mya was greatly impressed by the rain and brought forth many new kinds of life. Animas and Planas too, experienced a period of great creativity. Sometime between them, the humble Myxoty fungus was created, which is both plant and animal. Immediately Animas claimed it as her own, but Planas was greatly offended, having had much to do with its birth. The twins contended for quite some time and their dissention brought forth many new kinds of life. In the end, Mya sent forth the flowering plants which cannot live without the aid of insects such as bees, and both twins were placated.

The other gods thought it a great cleverness and Serros spoke, 'You rock, Mya.' We're still not sure exactly what that means.

There had been animosity for quite some time but still this was not the birth of wickedness.

Then one day, Waglah of the oceans desired to send a gift to Lumos for keeping time so well. Serros was put out by this, considering himself the god of the *laws* of time (which he isn't really) and so he sent a gift to Planas in honour of trees, knowing full well what effect this gift would have on his sister, Animas.

As he knew she would be, Animas was jealous. 'Has he seen not my great works?' she said and burst into tears. In her sorrow, she accidentally allowed some of her creatures into Waglah's domain that caused the goddess of the seas no end of strife, which was what Serros intended all along.

Animas spoke unto Waglah apologetically, as is written, 'Sorry, sorry, so sorry!' But Waglah tore herself with great storms in her discomfort and displeasure.

Pumos was annoyed at Serros for this cunning act that had caused so much trouble, and said to himself, 'What a towel' (or so it is written) then spoke to Waglah, 'Stay thine anger, 'tis not the fault of Animas.'

But Waglah spoke unkindly to him saying, 'Go stick a wet squirrel where Serros does not see.' (By this it is generally supposed to mean his armpits, but interpretations do differ...)

Pumos, greatly displeased, used his darkness to set a great vessel of rotten fish outside the front door of the god Serros in retribution. The next morning when Serros went to bring the sun to the world, the fish swam out and swarmed him with their stench.

Thus the jealous god Serros became greatly angered and was about to punish Waglah when Animas confessed it was actually Pumos who had done this. Serros refused to come out for three whole days, and in the darkness, Reicalg was born (lesser god of the cold).

Things were tense for a while, yet still wickedness was not born.

Many eons later, Serros proposed a great feast in honour of their creators Halm and Lallaellaia, both of whom were invited but neither of whom attended in

          By Dr Joseph Ireland "Dr Joe"

person. As it sometimes happened, Lumos was concerned about making everything 'just right' and managed to step on Animas' toes while she was in the kitchen. Somehow, the main meal was burned to a crisp and then everyone got *really* upset. Animas threw a spoon at Lumos, and Serros set fire to Pumos' napkin. Each god went to sulk in a separate corner of the world for a while.

Soon after Mya, in order to ease the tension brought about by the failure of the great feast, suggested that they all engage in a nice little project together that would require all their skills and keep them off each other's toes for a while. She suggested that maybe they could possibly consider at some point thinking about perhaps creating a race of beings that would be self-aware, if it weren't too much trouble, as they the gods were, and thus their creations would have the right to choose their own destiny and be quite the distraction to the sulking deity.

Then wickedness was born.

Each of the Elder gods immediately thought they *alone* could best build such a creation, and thus were born the leviathan of Waglah, the angels of Serros, the stars of Lumos, the fey beings of Planas, dragons of Animas, the shadow beings of Pumos, and giants of Mya. For a long time they fought great wars, wars which are still waged to this day. Amid this great animosity many new gods were born, such as Raag, the god of anger, Math, the terrible god of nightmares, and Kcha-Ka, the evil god of contention.

These new gods soon took the battle to a new level, inventing terrible weapons for the gods and their servants to use – nightmares, disease and guilt, just to name a few. The Elder gods, however, were immortal, and cared little for the death of their creations. As the battles continued, many other servant gods were born or created, such as Krigel, the mischief maker, who stole from the other gods; Kharm, the blade of justice, who punished those who crossed his path; and Nakuul, the terrible god of tar and pitch.

Eventually, Mya began to mourn for what she had caused, and brought forth a son, believed to be of Halm, and named him En-Saraph in the hope that he would bring light and peace to the warring world.

Tragically, En-Saraph chose evil instead of good, though he was a creature of both beauty and power. He became known as Neth, and he rallied the gods of evil and brought them against the Elder gods in a terrible battle, slaying many and never opening the house of his prisoners. In the process of time he too, with his lieutenant the monster god Oodri'aa, rose to become an Elder god.

Of the war of the gods and the rise of the demon lord Neth, Oath Master, much is written. It was at his bidding that that Pumos committed a great act of evil in the darkness and was banished by the other Elder gods into the far realm where he could work out his suffering. Now

By Dr Joseph Ireland "Dr Joe"

Pumos shepherds the souls of the dead to their place in the afterlife and keeps the souls of the wicked to punish them with eternal suffering.

Eventually Lallaellaia, taking pity on the warring gods, brought forth the Ancients. They were a tall race, twice the height of modern humans, and vastly intelligent. Their six thin limbs were surprisingly strong and it was said they could survive with comfort in any natural condition. Most of all, their minds were magical, and they could shape metal and carve stone with just a thought. It was these mighty and powerful creatures that eventually brought peace to the warring gods.

This peace lasted a long time, but it was a peace built on balance – that no one god should gain more power than the others. Together with the gods, they built the legendary city of *Civita Aurea* – the city of gold, and initiated a time of peace and prosperity never before seen on this world and perhaps never to be seen again. Eventually however, even the good and kind Ancients moved on from this world, leaving the gods behind. But before the Ancients left they too, tried their hand at creation, bringing forth all the sentient races of the humanoids – the humans, trolls, elves, dwarves, gnomes, goblins and many more.

For a long time, this fragile peace continued. Then, one day Serros found a lone human worshipping him. For a while, he wondered what the human was doing, till the god realised that from this worship he gained strength. He realised he could use this new strength to work miraculous acts of power in the world, and if one sentient gave him strength, he knew many would make him truly mighty.

Serros knew that if he did not use this new source of power immediately another god one day would, and then he would lose his advantage. So he immediately set about building a mighty religion to his name that gave him enormous power against all his enemies, of whom Neth and Pumos are the first.

Thus the first priests came into the world and religions were built by all the gods. The first faith, known as the Pantheon, contains the seven Elder gods we worship today and that must be worshipped every day or they may lose power and the gods of evil gain too much strength in the world. They are:

Serros – God of the sun, keeper of laws.
Lumos – Goddess of the moon, keeper of times.
Waglah – Goddess of the waters, keeper of knowledge.
Planas – God of plants, keeper of health and wealth.
Animas – Goddess of animals, keeper of love and war.
Pumos – God of darkness, keeper of the dead.
Mya – Goddess of the earth, keeper of life.

The hundred thousand (or so) lesser and servant gods

may be respected on occasion, but it is dangerous to allow them to take the place of the combined strength of the Pantheon. Neth and the evil gods must not be worshipped under any condition, for they reward their worshippers with eventual damnation and eternal suffering.

(Note – it is said that Halm, the ageless Overgod of time and his Overgodess wife, Lallaellaia, need no worshippers, for they are beyond our comprehension and cannot hear our prayers. But it is possible that the Elder gods themselves worship them.)

This is the true story of how the world began and what our place is within it. Worship the Pantheon and they will protect you. Send them your strength and one day they may banish the gods of evil to the silent realm of Pumos forever.

– by Aimhirghin Muirín, gnome historian.

The Pantheon of Elder Gods

Mya

11 Mya

Goddess of the earth, keeper of life.

Colour – red and brown.

Heavenly body – earth.

Servants – the giants.

Sacred weapon – club or sword.

Healing focus – bones and blood.

Zone of responsibility – earth, building and construction, unborn children.

Noted among human cultures for her patience and benevolence, Mya is often seen as punishing and whimsical in other cultures. Stories of her generally highlight her as profoundly wise and respectful of personal choice.

Mya has few priests, but is called on often as a kind of 'miscellaneous' god, perhaps because she also has the most offspring to command. Priests of Mya focus on stone craft and being helpful. They are stoic and dependable, but can be volcanic when moved to indignation.

Annas

12 Annas

By Dr Joseph Ireland "Dr Joe"

Goddess of animals, keeper of love and war.

Colour – orange.

Heavenly body – the orange star.

Servants – the dragons.

Sacred weapon – bow, claws.

Healing focus – muscles, motivation and creativity.

Zone of responsibility – animal life, family, adults and the newly married.

Annas is a curious deity, at times both extraverted and distant. She is recorded as taking the forms of a white field mouse or a fire breathing forest dragon. Often depicted as a young and healthy huntress, she has a hand in any affair involving animal life – so all of life in general. Paradoxically, or perhaps in evidence of greater wisdom, Annas fulfils the roles of both a cupid and a nemesis. Quick to liven thing up, she has been known to provoke change through almost any means, such as inspiring a whirlwind romance or inciting a deadly boarder skirmish. When her star moves near Mya the animal life is more abundant and livelier (about every two years). Annas is called on by both healers and hunters, known for both helping them personally, and pushing them to an inch of their lives simply to bring out their best. Her priests are wild and ferocious hunters at times, docile and placid shepherds at others. Both respect hard work and all forms of artistic expression, especially dance.

Serros

13 Serros

 By Dr Joseph Ireland "Dr Joe"

God of the sun, keeper of laws.

Colour – yellow and gold.

Heavenly body – the sun.

Servants – the angels.

Sacred weapon – flaming halberd.

Healing focus – mortal will, skin and digestion.

Zone of responsibility – the heavens, unwed youth, law.

Begrudgingly or otherwise, Serros is usually depicted as the foremost of the Elder gods. He is a strict keeper of laws, blessing both evil and good individuals as long as they obey the law. Known for occasional acts of benevolence, he is no fool and is quick to perceive law breaking and punish it. It was he who enacted the punishment on Pumos millennia ago. Serros is known for having a bit of a temper.

His yellow clad priests are the most common in the Great Kingdom, and are constantly being called on in matters of law and to enact punishment. Serros is represented in every known civilisation.

Planas

14 Planas

 By Dr Joseph Ireland "Dr Joe"

God of plants, keeper of health and family.

Colour – green.

Heavenly body – white star (brightest in the sky).

Servants – the fey beings.

Weapon – sickle or scythe.

Healing focus – healing in general, emotions.

Zone of responsibility – plant life, health, young children.

A soft-spoken deity, Planas is known as an enjoyer of simple pleasures. He is the twin to Annas and good friend of Mya. The white star is rumoured to be a beautiful world given over to plant life and its circuit near Mya marks out several minor patterns in her life as well. (As is stated, when Planas is near, no plant needs fear.)

The Priesthood of Planas tend to crops, fields and natural wilderness places, protecting each with religious fervour. The blessing of a priest of Planas should always be sought before planting, harvest, damming a river or building a structure out of wood (etc.). It is well recorded that many gifted or chosen of Planas, called to protect and serve a given natural site with supernatural power, are rarely humanoid. History has records of walking trees, men made out of pure water, and fire breathing deer.

Lumos

 By Dr Joseph Ireland "Dr Joe"

Goddess of the moon, keeper of times.
Colour – light blue and silver.
Heavenly body – the moon.
Servants – the stars.
Weapon – the sickle (and medical implements).
Healing focus – the voice, disease and immunity.
Zone of responsibility – the sky, truths and adulthood.

A supernaturally patient deity, also the oldest, born of her mother Lallaellaia and Halm. The Patient Keeper is as exact as her twin brother Serros, but far more merciful and tolerant, often keeping his desire for retribution in check with a kind word. Her vast knowledge of times gives her great understanding of equilibrium, medicines and prophecy. She is known as the gentle speaker; mediating between gods and humans at critical moments, balancing out passions and softly speaking a powerful truth at a key moment.

Her priesthood (mostly priestesses) includes many chatty individuals given to music and all other forms of artistic expression. They are as common, but less pronounced, as the priests of Serros. For them, a good life is just as rewarding as a great deed such as winning a battle. Some chosen of Lumos, while well aware of their calling, wear no sacred vestments or wield no weapons. They live apparently normal lives. They are, however, outspoken for various causes they and their deity agree on as important, and history records how apparently unremarkable individuals have single handily changed the course of kings with a well-timed and passionate speech.

Waglah

16 Waglah

 By Dr Joseph Ireland "Dr Joe"

Goddess of waters, keeper of mysteries.

Colour – dark blue.

Heavenly body – the far star (with four companions).

Servants – the leviathan.

Weapon – spear, fangs.

Healing focus – bodily liquids, the mind.

Zone of responsibility – the oceans, ageing and the old aged.

Waglah is the most mysterious and least understood of the Elder deities. She is treated as capricious, inscrutable; at times merciful, at other times whimsically destructive. It is suspected by some sages that she is poorly understood by even the other gods and at times feels quite lonely. Perhaps her immense knowledge is at times deeply troubling, driving her to destroy apparently innocent civilisations for the great evil they will one day unleash upon the world, and at times saving the life of an evil woman so that she may raise a noble prince. The other gods respect her and trust her wisdom greatly, since few beside her seem able to handle the weight of such understanding.

She has countless riverside and seashore shrines but priests are not so much employed as chosen. They operate outside a regular priesthood but can generally be found when needed. To see one lower his (or her) staff as a boat is launched is an ill omen. Sailors who pray to her note she is not easily placated and only sincere repentance, and throwing just about everything overboard (including sinners) presents only a small chance that she will sway her course.

Pumos

17 Pumos

 By Dr Joseph Ireland "Dr Joe"

God of darkness, secrets, and keeper of the dead.

Colour - dark purple and black.

Heavenly body – the deep star – furthest from Serros.

Servants – living shadows, the dead.

Weapon – a concealed blade.

Healing focus – our shadows (thus; destiny, according to some).

Zone of responsibility – nighttime, the dead (but also dreams).

Pumos is said to judge the condemned by awakening their conscience and confronting them with their sins, resulting in the worst kind of torment imaginable. He was once the foremost deity in *Civit Aurea* till thrown down by the others (especially Serros). Rumours hold he once was a royal purple and a god of higher truths, but now he loathes his own existence and is not capable of changing.

Pumos' priests share differing respect in different cultures, eclipsing even Serros in some. Generally, he is only prayed to at funerals for compassion for the deceased, and he seems to like it that way. His priests are considered ill omens but treated with almost the same amount of respect as the other priests of the pantheon. They dwell in darkness and, like their god, are practically friendless.

Other deities

Halm

Ageless Overdeity of time.

Colour - grey.

Heavenly body – none.

Healing focus – time, destiny, prophecy.

Zone of responsibility – all time and energy in creation, including purpose and meaning.

"The Uncaring" is a mysterious being that is considered beyond mortal comprehension. He appears to sponsor no direct worshippers, but may be worshipped by the Elder gods themselves. If he is aware of mortal's existence, he apparently doesn't care. It is understood he measures the exact time of every point within Creation from his observation tower that exists outside reality as we know it.

 By Dr Joseph Ireland "Dr Joe"

Lallaellaia

Ageless Overdeity of the universe.

Colour - typically black, with starlike sparkles and strange wispy clouds (the meaning of which is unknown).

Heavenly body – all of creation.

Healing focus – worlds / creation itself.

Zone of responsibility – all matter and space within creation.

Most scholars consider Creation – the stars, planets and everything in between and beyond, to be the physical manifestation of the goddess Lallaellaia herself. As an Overdeity it is unlikely she is aware of mortal existence, but may be worshipped by the Elder deity of the Pantheon. It is unclear from historical records if she is benevolent, uncaring, or simply unconcerned about mortal civilisations. Thus no reason is known why she does not hear the prayers of petitioners. It is assumed that when she gives birth, it is to entire pantheon. It seems she is married to Halm, though their relationship appears to be one of convenience since few other beings are able to perceive her existence. Either that, or they are actually the same being as some troll scholars have suggested.

Paradoxical, misunderstood, and incomprehensible, few bother trying to understand the silent Overdeity, and all those that persist succumb to madness eventually.

The Eternal

18 The circle of the Eternal

 By Dr Joseph Ireland "Dr Joe"

God of all things.

Colour - typically white, or a rainbow.

Heavenly body – unknown.

Weapon – unknown.

Healing focus – demons, poisons, general healing.

Zone of responsibility – everything?

Another paradoxical deity, worshippers claim the Eternal is the god of all things, including, by derivation, all other gods. Clearly supported by all good gods and respected by evil ones, this deity's place in Creation is still unclear. Some evidence suggests this deity was worshipped pre-eminently in *Civit Aurea*, although the only surviving evidence is a single speech given, reportedly, by the Eternal himself on the day the city was founded. Much irony and enigma surrounds this minor faith with a seemingly unbounded deity, which mystery is welcomely admitted by its adherents resulting in a religion that welcomes debate, reinterpretation of canon, and the pursuit of a personal path towards the divine. It is held that the most faithful of adherents are taught by divine messengers and other intangible beings, where they are given truths which are not for public sharing - resulting in further speculation about this open yet mysterious faith.

(Neth)

19 (Neth)

 By Dr Joseph Ireland "Dr Joe"

God of wickedness, oathmaster, liebringer, demons.

Colour – none, impossible darkness.

Heavenly body – unknown (some scholars speculate a throne orbiting beyond the throne of Pumos).

Weapon – twin firebrand whips.

Healing focus – none, stolen health.

Zone of responsibility – wickedness, demons.

An obsessive megalomaniac, it is a known fact that Neth seeks to replace Serros as the lead god of the Pantheon. A son of Mya, he is charged with bringing wickedness into the world shortly after creation. Once a prodigious and powerful deity, he now leads legions of demons and fallen beings from depravity to deeper depravity.

The less that is spoken of him, the better.

The measure of things

By Darrix, the paladin's squire. Prepared for the acceptance of squire-ship sermon. Draft 1, initial notes. 90.3.313 CY.

'And the prophet increased in wisdom and in statue, and in favour with god and man.' Words of Meros, sage of the Eternal, 'In Council of Greater Things, approximately 220 CY.

Since the day of High King Erell, our culture encourages heroes. It is believed that few have the calling or talent to become a true hero, perhaps barely one in every thousand births. But those who have a duty to help others. I believe each hero must develop their entire being if they want to achieve their life's purpose, otherwise no matter how gifted one may be in mighty strength, what good will they achieve if they fail in issues of reason or faith? Of course, this does not go for heroes alone but each person may well consider these areas as vital for balanced personal development. I reason, from the scripture given above, that the most

Note – smart people are considered 'wise' and are encouraged to be more than informative but also to make correct decisions. Knowing, but not doing, indicates you don't understand an issue at all. Perhaps that is why poorly educated individuals are considered unwise, not uneducated, and 'uneducated' means 'ill-mannered'.

          By Dr Joseph Ireland "Dr Joe"

important qualities that define a hero are as follows:

Wisdom (mental faculties – mind) Involves all mental facilities, from the ability to remember large numbers to the ability to make insightful decisions. It measures one's ability to solve problems, to see logic where others see only chaos. Wisdom is the province of the educated wizard, learned scholar, the skilled artisan. It is also the province of the master tactician, conniving prince or cunning rogue. It includes intelligence, education, memory, cognitive agility, battle planning, insight, cunning and intuition.

Stature (physical abilities – body) Includes physical prowess, health, stamina, endurance, and to a certain extent, will power. It is the province of the skilled soldier, brawling barbarian or silent assassin. In this world, the hulking fighter is at no advantage to the slim rogue.

Favour (social skills – social) Measures social ability, such as the ability to convince and influence others or your effect when you enter a room. It is the province of the smooth politician, swashbuckling rogue or master musician. Yet it is also the province of the feared criminal, the beguiling witch or the powerful sorceress.

Note – countless scholars have tried, and failed, to explain why those with enchanter powers are not only influential among others, but seem to use that same power to command the fields of magic that surround this world as well. Time will tell if their powers are divine, profane, or simply a natural phenomenon.

Those with this talent frequently display a profound

connection to the magic in the world, becoming enchanters, or simply being naturally adept at wielding items of known magical powers.

Grace (spiritual powers – spirit) This quality expresses an individual's closeness to the divine, seership and the ability to communicate with spirits. It is the power to communicate the will of the gods, predict their plans and interpret dreams. Perceived in some cultures as luck, even the unwise can be prodigious in this power. It is the province of the devout priestess, profane assassin or the propitious rogue.

Note – a similar discourse was delivered many years ago by King Dunnkan's father King Peyter, rest his soul. He died at 50, half the age a king should reach (and half the age of his father, King Wolace).

A simple example: Studious and well educated, Piex handles the role of informant and councillor with wizardry and educated advice willingly given at all times. Broad and muscular, Posk the young half troll carries the group's need for raw muscle with obedience and dedication. Allastassia, well-travelled and dominant in all social interactions, pre-empts almost all the group's social needs and handles alliances with exceptional talent. And I often find myself, somewhat

Note – it is not clear where Kialessa, the tae'anaryn, fits at the moment. She's talented at everything, constantly surprising me with her rapid ability to learn and overcome new tasks. Perhaps she truly is just good at everything? Time will tell.

devoted and apparently gifted in matters divine, called on to pray for healing and protection for the group.

This may be illustrated in the following image;

20 The four virtues

In the end, the attributes do not determine the heroes, the hero must determine which attributes they focus on to define themselves. It is their deeds that make them who they are, not arbitrary qualities such as these. My point here today is to demonstrate that one reason heroes become great is because many of them will focus on their *whole being*, not neglecting one area of weakness simply because they have an impressive strength.

Yet I believe we *all* have great tasks to fulfil. You may not be called to slay a fell dragon, but you may indeed raise someone who will. In the day of their infancy they will need you. If you are weak in one area of your life you, like any hero of old, may fail in your duty. Or just as worse, fail to prepare them for theirs. I tell you these things today because I feel inspired to encourage you to work on honing each of these four key areas, not only so that we may fulfil the purpose for which we are intended, but also because I believe that when we are healthy, surrounded by the right kind of people, properly educated and inspired by the divine…

… we will also be happy.

I know where you are coming from, young squire, but this is more informative than inspirational. I think you'd better come and talk to me before you attempt to rewrite this sermon, honoured gentle Darrix. – Tomin.

 By Dr Joseph Ireland "Dr Joe"

Join in!

Connect to other readers.

Come share your experiences at

www.DrJoe.id.au

and check out our other great books at

www.CreatingScience.Org

By Dr Joseph Ireland "Dr Joe"

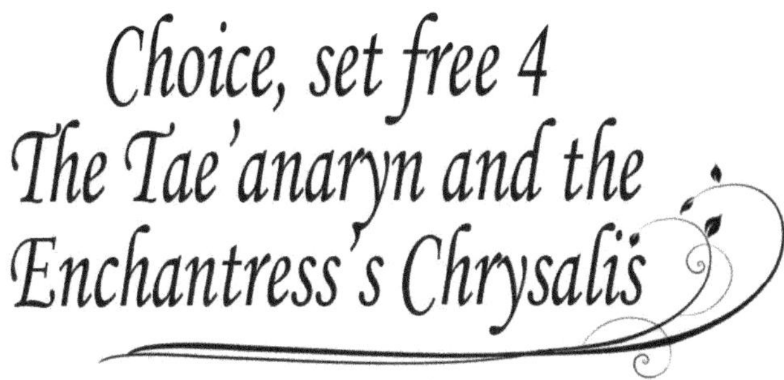

Choice, set free 4
The Tae'anaryn and the Enchantress's Chrysalis

Allastassia: Talented, beautiful, powerful.

But is it enough?

Life is complex; people love, people disagree, people change.

And sometimes people do things they deeply regret…

By Dr Joseph Ireland "Dr Joe"   231

By Dr Joseph Ireland "Dr Joe"

Choice, Set Free

The Tae'anaryn & the Paladin's Squire

 By Dr Joseph Ireland "Dr Joe"

Choice, Set Free

Place the date and your personal mark here each time you read this book – libraries included!

Why not share your experiences and thoughts with the fandom! Get a grownup's permission and visit

www.DrJoe.id.au

for fan art, sequels, competitions and more!

 By Dr Joseph Ireland "Dr Joe"